THE DUCHESS OF DRURY LANE

MILLIONAIRES OF MAYFAIR

JANNA MACGREGOR

The Duchess Of Drury Lane
Copyright © 2023 Janna MacGregor
Cover Art by Forever After Romance Designs

eBook License Notes:

Disclaimer: This is a work of fiction. Names, characters, places, and incidents are products of the author's imagination, or the author has used them fictitiously.

CHAPTER ONE

Drury Lane
London

For most theatre lovers, the opportunity to have a private tour of Drury Lane would definitely be preferable to having a tooth pulled. However, this was not the case for Miss Celeste Worsley, who stood outside the noble theatre alongside Alice Cummings.

If Celeste's grandfather found out that Alice was carrying a baby, he'd have her thrown into the street before Celeste could utter a word in her maid's defense.

Since the first day she'd stepped into her grandfather's house, he had repeatedly warned Celeste that under no circumstances could she bring scandal, dishonor, or embarrassment to the family name.

Yet, two simple words, such as "I'm carrying," foretold a drama that would rival a new play in Drury Lane. Celeste would do everything in her power to protect Alice from her grandfather, and anyone else who might humiliate her maid. The truth was that Alice wasn't just a lady's maid.

She was Celeste's friend and had been ever since Celeste's mother had first employed her.

"Alice, how did this happen?" Celeste bit her tongue to keep from cursing. Alice's stomach had become fuller, but Celeste had attributed it to the fact that she always asked her friend to share breakfast with her in her bedroom. It had been a godsend when Alice had agreed. It meant she didn't have to face her grandfather's inquisition about her friends or her parents' letters.

The maid's plump cheeks blossomed into a color that would make poppies jealous. "Well, Miss, you know about the birds and the bees. Not to mention his and her bits and how they fit together."

Celeste lifted her palm. "That's not what I meant. How did you and Benjamin…er…find the time and place?"

Alice chuckled. "That's easily explained. Benjamin's employer, Mr. Hollandale—"

"Wait, for goodness' sake," Celeste hissed. "*Mr. Malcolm Hollandale?*"

Alice nodded. "He's such a nice man."

Celeste couldn't attest to his pleasant personality. She'd barely said two words to the man, but she had studied him at every society event they attended together. It wasn't an exaggeration to say that she was an expert on his stunningly handsome good looks, the impeccably tailored evening clothes he wore, and how the skin around his captivating sapphire eyes crinkled when he laughed. Tall, blond, and ruggedly gorgeous described him perfectly.

Most of the *ton* considered him the perfect male specimen. But they refused to overlook one simple fact. He was not an aristocrat nor a member of the landed gentry. He was a man of trade. He might be a self-made millionaire and a member of the Duke of Pelham's rarified Millionaires Club, but those facts didn't change anyone's haughty opinion regarding the man.

But Celeste had never cared a whit about that, nor had her heart. It tumbled anew into infatuation every time she saw him. But she had warned that traitorous organ repeatedly—it could gaze to its *heart's content,* but there was to be no engagement.

Alice nodded as if she was privy to Celeste's private thoughts. "Mr. Hollandale allows us to visit in Benjamin's rooms whenever we have time together. They are over Mr. Hollandale's laboratory." She shrugged with a sheepish smile. "We might have gotten a bit enthusiastic during a few of our visits."

"I see," Celeste said. Enthusiastic was an understatement. She patted her maid's arm. "No matter what comes from our conversation today, I'll help you find a way to be with your Benjamin."

"If he doesn't marry me, I'll be ruined." Her maid's throat bobbed when she swallowed, the movement betraying her fear. "I can't go home, Miss. My mam will disown me."

"It won't come to that. Everything you've told me about your Benjamin leads me to believe he'll welcome you and the baby." Several inches taller than her maid, Celeste bent her knees until her gaze met Alice's teary brown eyes. "Trust me?"

When Alice nodded, Celeste took her maid's hand and tugged her up the front steps. "Why is Benjamin here today?"

"Mr. Hollandale's experiment failed, so they must remove it."

Celeste stilled. "They?"

"Ben and Mr. Hollandale," Alice offered.

Celeste hardened her stomach. No matter what

happened, her first and only concern was for Alice and her baby. She could not...would not...spend her precious time mooning over Malcolm Hollandale.

It made little difference that every part of her body seemed to tingle when she looked at him.

Without wasting another second, Celeste opened the theatre door and escorted Alice inside. As soon as they stepped into the main auditorium, it appeared that they'd entered a busy beehive. Workers milled around the stage while the pounding of hammers echoed throughout the theatre. A man shouted directions as he pointed at a drawing in his hands.

But none of it caught Celeste's interest. Her eyes were focused on Malcolm Hollandale, the bane of her existence. It wasn't that he was rude or ignored her. Quite the opposite. Whenever she'd seen him at a *ton* event, he had been most courteous to her and everyone else. But Celeste couldn't concentrate on anything or anyone else when he was in the room. Consequently, men thought her standoffish. She wasn't. She was simply under Malcolm Hollandale's spell. Thankfully, he had no idea about her true feelings.

She'd be horrified if he ever discovered that she was totally and irrevocably in love with him. That proved her heart hadn't listened to any of her warnings about looking but not engaging.

Alice bounced on her toes as she raised her hand in a wave. All Celeste's attention was focused on Malcolm Hollandale, but then a man on his hands and knees stood and waved back.

Celeste bent her head and released a deep breath. She had to get ahold of herself. Alice wasn't waving at Hollandale. She was waving at the young man working next to him, who must be Benjamin. Celeste would do well to remember that the world didn't revolve around Mr. Hollandale.

Benjamin said something to Malcolm, who nodded. As Alice's beau approached them, Celeste stood still like a rabbit caught by a fox's penetrating stare. Malcolm's eyes were locked on hers for a moment that surely lasted an hour. What kind of a man who was graced by the gods' own hands and looked like Apollo worked as a common laborer?

A very real, but very sweaty Malcolm Hollandale.

Her cheeks grew unbearably hot, but she refused to turn away. Her grandfather was the Duke of Exehill. It was one of the oldest titles in the British Isles, and she'd always been taught never to lower her gaze to anyone.

And that included a devilishly handsome man who made her heartbeat accelerate faster than a thoroughbred at the Royal Ascot. She should know fast horses. Her father bred and sold them to peers, their heirs, other sons, and anyone else who was mad about the creatures.

Hollandale smirked when she'd lifted her chin. Without second-guessing her cause, she marched straight toward him. If her plan had any hopes of succeeding, she needed Malcolm Hollandale's help.

And Malcolm Hollandale needed her.

He just didn't know it yet.

On his hands and knees scrubbing away his latest attempt at creating a hardwood floor varnish, Malcolm Hollandale didn't know whether he was more frustrated that his failed varnish had turned into a sticky mess or the fact that he was sweating as if he were attending a smithy's fire.

"Ack, Hollandale, I'm sorry I had to ask you to remove it." Florizel Holland, the theatre's stage manager, scratched his head as he grimaced at the floor. "If this exact spot weren't where we mark the actor's positions for tonight's performance, I would tell you to leave it until the new production begins." He shrugged.

Malcolm stopped. "Thank you, but that would be too dangerous. If one of your actors stepped in this exact spot, I'm afraid they'd be stuck until the final curtain."

"It might help a few of them. Some of the actors don't know how to stand still when they deliver their lines." Florizel smiled. "I appreciate you coming so quickly. If you continue sanding at that speed, we will not have to miss rehearsal today."

"Florizel," someone called.

"You're popular today," Malcolm quipped.

"I always am when there are problems." Florizel nodded at the understudy who called him. "I'll bid you farewell."

"Mr. Hollandale?" Benjamin Brannan stopped his work and sat on his haunches. He pointed at two women. "It's my Alice. She's been feeling poorly lately." He turned and waved at her. "May I—"

"Go," Malcolm said, not wasting a second. "I'm the one who created this mess. I should be the one to clean it."

"Thank you, sir," Benjamin said as he rose to his feet.

Malcolm smiled at the young man. Ben had been working beside Malcolm for nearly two years and was one of the hardest-working employees Malcolm had ever had the good fortune to hire. So, whenever Benjamin asked for a break, Malcolm never refused him.

He continued to sand away on the floor but slowed his motion when he noticed Celeste Worsley's fragrance wafting in the air around him, which was amazing since the entire theatre could host over three-thousand-six-hundred visitors at a time. Yet even in such a cavernous space, he knew the exact moment she'd entered the building.

She stood back from the stage and seemed to be comforting Alice, the lady's maid whom Benjamin had taken a fancy to. Ben and Alice were from the same small town. Malcolm would wager that the two of them would marry if Alice could be convinced to give up her position as Celeste Worsley's maid.

Malcolm had met Miss Celeste Worsley over a year ago at a *ton* event. Even though she was the very definition of an incomparable beauty who possessed excellent poise and deportment, he always detected censure in her gaze when she looked upon him. For some unknown reason, she'd taken an instant dislike to him and had never bothered to hide her contempt. She always smirked, although slightly, whenever she glanced in his direction.

As Malcolm stole a peek, he sighed. She wore her typical expression of disapproval.

It aggravated him to no end. Her parents were the definition of scandal. He'd wager that their daughter was on a first-name basis with scandalous behavior. The apple never falls far from the tree and all that. He wiped the sweat out of his eyes. For God's sake, he was one of the rare millionaires of Mayfair. Alas, there were only a select few peers he considered friends. Though, his friends had no trouble accepting him for who he was, an inventor with impeccable manners. They were the rare exception. Most people could not ignore his humble upbringing despite his wealth.

Including Celeste Worsley. Though a mere viscount's daughter, she walked and talked as if she were a duchess in her own right. He chuckled, wondering what she'd think of the moniker he'd given her. She'd likely scowl even more if she knew that he called her the Duchess of Drury Lane.

As he continued to sand the sticky varnish from the floor, Malcolm stole another glance in her direction. He slowed the repetitive sanding motion while tracking her movements but leaned his weight into the work.

As Celeste held her head high, she walked as if she indeed were a duchess. If it were anyone else, he'd smile in welcome, but it was Celeste Worsley in all her judgmental glory. Even if she did think she was better than any other human, he couldn't deny that watching her was one of his favorite pastimes.

He returned to staring at his hands but knew the moment when she was before the stage. Less than ten feet separated them.

"Mr. Hollandale? I wonder if I might have a word with you."

Her sweet voice twisted itself around his chest and squeezed like a clinging vine, robbing him of breath. For the love of heaven, even his cock took notice and twitched at the sound. How could a woman such as she cause all his logic and intelligence to take its leave?

"Mr. Hollandale?" she repeated.

This time at the sound of his name, he pushed all of his weight into the sandpaper. That's when he heard the sound of the wood creaking and cracking beneath him.

"Mr. Hollandale, you're bleeding."

He looked down to see a splinter the size of a one-hundred-year-old elm stuck in the middle of his palm. It didn't register what was happening until the excruciating throbbing struck him with the force of a hurricane.

"*Bloody hell!*" Pure instinct drove Malcolm to shake his hand as if that would dislodge the offending tree. Blood trailed down his arm. He pulled his hand to his chest. For a moment, he was afraid he would cast up his accounts from the pain.

"Let me help."

When he looked up, he couldn't believe the sight before him. Somehow, Celeste had climbed onto the stage and reached for his hand.

"There's no need," he said brusquely.

"There's every need," she said, not paying a whit of attention to his curtness. "You're bleeding, and I have a clean handkerchief at my disposal."

Like a wounded animal, he flinched when she reached for his hand.

"I have suffered splinters myself. They can become quite nasty if you don't clean the wound and dig out the irritating piece of wood." Instead of chiding him for acting like a child, she soothed him. "Do you suppose there's any brandy around?" She laughed. "What am I saying? There must be. This is a theatre, after all. Actors are notorious for insisting upon only serving the finest brandy in such an establishment." She leaned close and lowered her voice. "I dare say that you and I could use a little tipple ourselves after this day. Come with me."

Tipple? What lady of good breeding used that term?

Who was this woman standing before him, and what had she done with the incredibly proper and enormously conceited Celeste Worsley?

CHAPTER TWO

T ipple? What possessed her to say such a nonsensical word? It was a word her great aunt would use before she went back for thirds at the Christmastide punch bowl.

"Did you say tipple?" Malcolm asked in all his sweaty gorgeousness as he towered over her. Beads of sweat trailed the sides of his face. His matted blond hair appeared brown from all the dampness. If he were anyone else, she'd likely be repulsed, but with him, she wanted to inhale his scent, bathe in it, then perhaps bottle it to enjoy later.

His large blue eyes twinkled in such a way that they appeared to be the color of the finest turquoise outlined in blue sapphires. His high cheekbones, perfectly straight nose, and the brown brows that framed his eyes were perfection. He was so beautiful that an artist would drool over him. She wasn't an artist but could appreciate beauty when she saw it. He was the type of man who would command a ladies' auxiliary meeting to silence just by walking into the room. He was that handsome.

She held his hand in hers as he watched her every

move. His lips twitched with a smile that immediately softened his features.

For the love of heaven, she'd never been this close to him. His mouth was less than six inches from hers. If she stood on tiptoe, she could kiss those plump lips that begged to be bitten. Instead, she bit her own lip to remind herself that she had to help him and then ask for a favor. But frankly, it was difficult to form a rational thought, let alone speak it aloud when the man she'd loved from afar was mere inches from her.

"Perhaps you didn't hear me, *Your Grace*," he chided playfully. He winked as if he knew what type of effect he had on her. "Tipple?"

Celeste shook her head in a desperate attempt to clear the muddle and the *tipple* from her mind. That's when the name finally sunk in.

"What did you call me?"

If possible, his eyes gleefully sparkled a little more. "Your Grace. That's what I've always called you."

"Why?" Without even considering what she was doing, she squeezed his hand.

He grimaced slightly.

"Pardon me," she murmured.

He nodded once as if decreeing all was forgiven. "You love to attend the theatre. And when you walk in, I know the moment you arrive. You have an air about you that orders mere mortals to look at you." He shrugged but continued to smile.

His grin was nothing more than a gloat in her opinion. They were currently standing inside the stage manager's office, where they'd managed to find a bottle of brandy. Without tearing her gaze from his and certainly without any warning, she splashed a good amount on his hand.

"What the devil, woman!" Malcolm shook his hand as if it were on fire, then hissed in pain.

Calmly, she said, "That's your punishment for calling me conceited."

He shook his injured hand once more but wore a contrite expression. "I apologize. I shouldn't have been so forthcoming in my pet names. It's not because you're aloof per se, but because of who you are."

She narrowed her eyes and glared at him. "And who am I?"

"I thought you knew." He laughed softly as he took a step toward her. "You're Miss Celeste Worsley. Your mother is the daughter of the Duke of Exehill. And your father is Viscount Worsley."

She blinked but didn't move otherwise. Where was the man she'd thought perfect?

He lowered his voice. "You enjoy the social Season and are considered quite popular." He looked over his shoulders as if he didn't want to be overheard. "You were declared a diamond of the first water during your introduction to society. They still say it's true."

"Is that what *they* say? I wouldn't know," she answered curtly. She wanted to roll her eyes at the word *they*, that ubiquitous group whom no one claimed to be a part of. To make matters worse, his voice reminded her of a tomcat's contented purr when it had just finished its evening meal of a fat mouse. She expected a thank you from the ungrateful *man* after ensuring that there were no lingering slivers of wood embedded in his palm. Frankly, his manners were as suspect as his teasing.

"Well, I concur with society's opinion of you," he said with a grin.

As if she cared what society thought of her. She only cared about what her grandfather thought of her. His good opinion was what she was working toward. She stepped toward the door to see where her lady's maid had run off to. For a moment, Celeste thought to leave but straightened her shoulders. She would not leave Alice in a lurch.

"Don't." With his good hand, he gently clasped her arm. "Don't leave. I want my tipple with *you*." The dastardly man had lowered his voice again, much like a lover would. "Why are you here?" Without a care in the world, he poured a fingerful of brandy into two glasses and handed one to her. "If I didn't know better, I'd say you're here to see me."

She opened her reticule and retrieved a clean handkerchief. "Wrap this around your wound." She held it out to him, and naturally, her hand shook slightly, betraying her nervousness. This was her punishment for forming an attachment to Mr. Malcolm Hollandale even if the clod didn't know it. If she'd been any type of a nurse, she would have wrapped his hand herself.

He lifted his glass in the air. "To our hearts' desires."

She did the same as she looked longingly toward the door. It shouldn't come as a surprise that he thought so poorly of her. Most of the *ton* knew her situation and made fun at her expense, but they had the good sense to do it behind her back. She wasn't exaggerating, nor was she an outsider per se. She was fine to sit next to at dinner parties and made an acceptable partner for the occasional waltz. Celeste could always be counted on to attend other mundane social activities to make the numbers even.

Yet she still felt like an outsider.

Her looks were fair, but men were more likely to hand her back to her chaperone after a dance than linger with her because they wanted her company.

But she never complained and always did what her grandfather told her. He used his wealth and position like a cudgel to ostracize people who didn't obey him. Her mother was a perfect example. She'd fallen in love with a mere viscount instead of marrying the man Celeste's grandfather had chosen for her.

Celeste had been a dutiful granddaughter and had tried hard to win her grandfather's affection and praise. He would soon choose a man for her to marry, one worthy of her bloodline, as her grandfather liked to remind her. Perhaps she should be happy to allow her grandfather to make her a match. It seems she was incapable of doing it herself. This made her third Season with no beau in sight desperate to win her regard.

There was never any question that Celeste would do as commanded. It was the only way that she could mend the rift that had torn her family apart. Her grandfather owned the mortgage on her father's estate. It was a small fortune. When a fire swept through the stables, he had no one to ask for the money. Banks refused his requests. Miraculously, her grandfather agreed to lend her father the funds to rebuild.

Her father's business still suffered from the fire, but little by little, things were improving. Once the mortgage was retired, Celeste had no doubt her father and mother's finances would be fine, and they'd live comfortably. But until then, Celeste would worry.

She blew out a breath. Right now, her worry was for Alice. She'd not leave this room without receiving Malcolm Hollandale's agreement to her request. It was for Alice's benefit. Her lady's maid needed her now, and Celeste would do everything in her power to help the woman she considered more like family than a servant.

Throughout Celeste's young adulthood, Alice had been the one to comfort her when people whispered behind her back that she was as wild and untamable as her mother.

Not to mention, she was nothing like her well-respected grandfather. The *ton* had warned that her reputation would be in tatters by the end of her first Season. But Celeste had proven them wrong. She had done everything she could to make her grandfather proud of her and would continue to do so.

That meant she'd possibly marry without love even if she believed and dreamt of it. But that sacrifice would be worth it. Her grandfather had promised her that he would forgive the mortgage if she married the man of his choosing. She hoped that meant that he'd ask her parents to London for the announcement of her betrothal and perhaps a reconciliation. If she couldn't have love, then at least she would be helping her parents.

"What's yours?" he asked.

"My what?" she fired back.

He chuckled at the hint of anger in her voice. "Testy, aren't we? I meant, what is your heart's desire?"

"Sir, I may have tended to your wound, but that doesn't mean we're intimates or even confidants." She tilted her chin as she shook her head. The gesture set the appropriate tone between them.

"Well, when you hold my hand and stroke your fingers across my palm, it makes me think we're more than just strangers," he hummed.

The sound vibrated in her chest. She drew a deep breath as heat set her cheeks aflame. It was the type of heat that told too much. The man might actually think she cared about his good opinion.

That was the problem with infatuations. When you were with the person you were besotted with, they usually disappointed you. The man in front of her was the perfect example of that theorem.

"Mr. Hollandale, you're too daring."

"Am I?" He grinned, then tutted. "Your eyes say otherwise. They flash when I tease you, indicating that you do indeed like my attention."

She huffed out a breath. "And you watch my every move." It was a bold thing to say, but she didn't flinch. "You're fascinated with me."

"You know me so well," he countered with a smile. "*I am* fascinated by you. Tell me why you're here besides"—he leaned close—"to spend time with me."

Beneath the humor in his eyes, there was assessment. He seemed to always evaluate her as if she were an experiment and he was waiting for her to fail. That was why she turned away first whenever he looked at her like he was right now.

"I left a glove here last night." She looked around the office. "I thought that the stage manager might have found it."

Malcolm narrowed his eyes. "There was no performance last night. Try again, duchess."

She bit the inside of her cheek at the word duchess. Why did she even lie? Every time she did, she was caught. "Alice wanted to visit."

She stared into his eyes, gathering the courage to ask the unthinkable. Though he treated her abominably, he was a good employer. According to Alice, he treated his employees with respect and paid them fair wages. She'd best tell him what she wanted before he charmed the stockings off her, making her forget why she came here.

"The real reason I'm here is that I want you to hire my lady's maid."

It was wicked of him, but he could not resist the opportunity to tease Miss Worsley. By the telltale flush of her cheeks and the brilliant flash in her emerald eyes, he had her full attention. He'd been raised to never anger a lady, but with the duchess, it seemed that teasing was the only way she'd let that proverbial armor slip and reveal bits and pieces of her real self.

"The real reason I'm here is that I want you to hire my lady's maid."

He froze, much like the statue of Achilles in his courtyard. Of course, he didn't have an arrow in his heel, but her words had a similar consequence.

"I beg your pardon, but I didn't hear you correctly." He shook his head once to break the spell between them, then leaned in closer to inhale her rose perfume. It was his favorite flower, and naturally, this prickly woman wore the scent to torture him. The set of her jaw reminded him of the sharp, curved thorns that were designed to protect the lovely bloom.

When she bit her lip and stared at the ground, it was the first indication of her unease. But she took a steely breath and lifted her gaze to his. "I would like you to hire Alice Cummings, my lady's maid."

"Why the devil do I need a lady's maid?" The curt words slipped free.

Her gorgeous green eyes widened, emphasizing the long silky lashes. Then she quickly narrowed her eyes and pursed her lips in a mulish expression. "Because your man, Benjamin Brannan impregnated Alice." Celeste swallowed, but she never looked away. "Alice will be ruined. They must marry. It'll be easier if she's in your household."

The air escaped his lungs, and he rested one hip on

Florizel's desk. "Ben never mentioned a word," he muttered.

"He didn't know. Alice is telling him now." Celeste came next to him and rested her perfect backside against the desk. She stared at her clasped hands. "She can't stay with me. The baby is showing, and my grandfather..." She closed her eyes, tilted her head to the ceiling, and then turned away.

An overwhelming urge to comfort her became nigh near impossible to ignore. But Malcolm refused to embarrass Celeste or make her more uncomfortable. She wouldn't welcome his touch anyway, even if it were offered as a comfort.

"Your grandfather?"

She faced him as she wiped a surprising tear from her cheek. The sight made him want to fix whatever was wrong and banish the sadness that dulled her green eyes.

"My grandfather would terminate her employment and throw her out into the street." She clenched and unclenched her fists. "I can't continue to have her with me for fear of what would happen. You have an excellent reputation for being a good and fair employer. I know that Benjamin lives with you—"

"He lives in several rooms above my workshop in the building I own," Malcolm corrected. "It's between Russell Square and Covent Gardens."

"That makes it easier if he doesn't live with you." She bit her lower lip, then nodded as if coming to some agreement with herself. "If they marry, and you're amenable, Alice could move in with Ben." She lowered her voice. "May I ask what his wages are? If need be, I can supplement his income with my pin money. I don't want either to suffer because of their circumstances." Her hands fluttered, revealing how distraught she was. "I just want Alice to be happy and safe. She believes she can have a happy life with Benjamin." She lifted her gaze to his. "May I ask a question? Is he a good man? Do you think he'll marry her?"

"That's two questions, but I'm feeling generous today." He winked.

She quirked an eyebrow. "Was that supposed to be humorous?"

Malcolm rubbed his neck. Now, she would think him flippant. "Forgive me. I don't mean to make light of the situation."

She blinked twice in response, never cracking a smile.

He cleared his throat. "He's the best of men. Hardworking, responsible, and kind. However, I'll not take your money. I can afford to help Ben and Alice."

Celeste nodded and then started to pace. "If he doesn't marry her, I don't know what I'll do." She stopped and turned to him. "You see, Alice has loved him since they were children. They grew up together."

Without thinking, he crossed the room and touched her arm to stop her pacing. "Hush. You're distressing yourself." Then he remembered how he must smell and pulled away from her. "I apologize for my forwardness. I must reek."

She shook her head, and a slight grin appeared. "Your scent is rather pleasant. Sandalwood?"

"Along with sweat." He ran a hand through his hair. "I don't think you have to worry about Ben marrying Alice. He'll take Alice's situation seriously."

"Can you help convince him if he doesn't?" Her voice had softened. "If you help them, I'll help you."

The devil himself must have spit out his next words. "You'll help me with what?"

The look of relief on her face kept him from retracting

the words. "I've always found that mutually beneficial bargains are in everyone's best interests." She nodded with a smile. "I will help you find a wife."

He almost choked on the words as he stumbled back a step. "A wife?"

Celeste nodded. "Everyone knows that you want to marry into the *ton*. I have the credentials and the acquaintances to make that happen."

He had been looking for a wife, a woman familiar with society's customs and etiquette. If he wanted to expand his business he needed to entertain, and a wife was essential to his cause. Truthfully, he wanted a wife for more important reasons, such as companionship. He sought a partner who would break the infinitely dull dreariness he faced when working long hours. He wanted a wife who wanted to spend time with him even if they were lost in their respective work.

He'd always been able to work, but lately, he'd felt off and unsettled until he realized he was suffering from loneliness. Two years ago, he had decided to find a woman and court her, but all the society misses just turned their backs on him. He might be gentry, but barely. His father was a poor vicar. Consequently, no one of good standing within the *ton* wanted to consider marriage with him.

He stared at her as if she had three heads. Surely, she wasn't making fun of him at his expense.

Celeste returned his stare, then lifted a perfectly arched brow in challenge.

He released a long-suffering sigh. "I know that look. You give it to me every time you see me. It reminds me of offal."

"Offal?" she sputtered.

"Indeed," he replied. "I know how society sees me. They think of me as a fortune hunter, but that's the opposite of what I want. I'm a wealthy man in my own right, but the *ton* doesn't see me as worthy of their time or friendship. Yet, they use my inventions practically every day."

"Meaning?"

"I created the glazes that keep their best china spotless and looking brand new." Now he was the one to tip his nose in the air.

The lives of all those snobs would be entirely different if it weren't for him. The glaze he created ensured no pockmarks or pits in the china itself, safeguarding the plate and the food served on it. If you ate beef one night, Malcolm's glaze ensured that the fish you ate the next night would not be contaminated by the previous night's meal.

"And I created a glaze that keeps tile and other ceramics protected. I'm currently working on a varnish for wooden floors."

She bit her lip to keep from smiling and nodded vigorously. "I'm well aware of your talents, sir. Indeed, I was talking with Lady Amelia Windhorst the other day about what our life would be like without the china shining brilliantly on the dining room table."

"Now you're making a jest at my expense." He tried to sound gruff, but he couldn't resist her. He sighed slightly. Why couldn't she treat him like this when they met at various societal events instead of avoiding him as if he were the plague?

"Now, I must apologize." She held out her hand. "I can introduce you to my friends and sing your praises."

He took her hand and shook it, sealing their bargain. "If you can do that, I can do the rest."

"Meaning?" She lifted a perfectly arched brow.

"I can charm my future wife with wit and my conversational abilities." He waggled his eyebrows. "And of course, my graceful dance moves."

"Oh, naturally," she mocked him with a smile. "Every person I know believes a potential marriage partner's athletic ability when performing a country line dance is critical to a successful marriage." She scoffed slightly. "I myself consider it a necessity in a husband." She bit her lip, but it didn't stop her laughter from escaping.

He couldn't help but join in her glee. Once their laughter died, he leaned near as if divulging a secret. "I also have other traits that would make me an excellent husband for someone."

"And what would those be?" she asked as a rogue giggle escaped.

"We'd have to be somewhere more private than this for me to show you."

Her eyes widened in shock as quiet exploded around them.

Had he spouted those words? It sounded as if he were propositioning her to an affair. What was it about the young woman before him that made him forget all his manners? "Forgive me for being crude."

The shocked look on her face quickly melted into a knowing smile as she held up her hand to stop him from continuing. "I look forward to you showing me more, Mr. Hollandale."

As the air suddenly crackled between them, they stood motionless before one another. Before today, they were enemies, at best, antagonists. Now, they were equals. He lifted his hand to cup her cheek but slowly lowered it. The urge to kiss her was nigh near impossible to ignore. However, now was not the time for a kiss. Not when he smelled like a barnyard. No, he'd wait for a more opportune time, then show her how he could kiss her until she didn't know her name. Undoubtedly, she would have the same effect on him.

Either that, or she'd deliver a well-deserved slap to his face.

"I look forward to that opportunity also, Miss Worsley." A smile tugged at one side of his mouth. Miss Celeste Worsley was flirting with him, a sight rarer than a full eclipse of the sun.

Before he could say more, Florizel entered the room. "Sorry to interrupt, but how long will you be? I have to meet my carpenter, Samantha Billings."

Celeste's gaze was glued to his. "I think we're done here."

"Thank you, Florizel," Malcolm called out.

The stage manager nodded, then started a conversation with one of his employees who'd come to ask him a question.

As the theatre burst into a new wave of activity, Malcolm didn't even think about the ramifications of inviting this charming woman into his workshop. How could he have ever considered her anything other than enchanting was beyond him? Today, she'd shown a side of herself that he couldn't resist.

And he didn't want to.

"Come to my workshop tomorrow. Alice can visit Benjamin, and we'll finish our conversation without fear of interruption."

CHAPTER THREE

"Ben was ever so excited when I told him the news," Alice gushed the next day. "He told me he was overjoyed. Then he kissed me and dropped to one knee. It was so romantic." She shook her head. "I can't believe that I'll be married to him. I love him so much." She sighed happily as she placed a hand on her stomach. "He told me the same and that he loves our baby already."

Celeste reached across the carriage and patted Alice's knee. She had heard this story at least twenty times since they'd returned from the theatre. She didn't begrudge Alice her happiness one bit. If there was anyone who deserved to have a happy future, it was Alice.

Her maid peeked out the window. "What did your grandfather say when you told him the news?" She frowned. "I'm sure he was angry."

"How could he be angry?" Especially since Celeste didn't dare tell him.

Alice looked at her askance.

If Celeste's grandfather were aware of Alice's condition, she'd be on the street. The same thing had happened to her mother, and her grandfather had cut her out of his life faster than a knife could cut a boiled potato.

Since Celeste had lived at her grandfather's London mansion during the Season, she tried to keep her conversation with her grandfather as innocuous as possible. It made her living arrangement much easier, especially since her parents never visited. But she corresponded with them every week. Everyone knew that her grandfather would not allow her mother to step inside his London home. Since her parents didn't have the money for Celeste's entrance into society, her grandfather unexpectedly agreed to host Celeste in her first Season. He was pleased with the arrangement and continued to host her in the subsequent years.

Though she lived with him, he didn't seem to care what she did during the days. For instance, today, she'd told him that she had a bit of shopping to do, then said she planned to call upon her good friend Lady Amelia Windhorst. He'd nodded in agreement, but she had no doubt that he hadn't paid any attention to what she was saying. He didn't care what she did as long as she kept her reputation intact.

Thankfully, Amelia had an unmarked black carriage with loyal coachmen who wore plain clothes. Amelia allowed Celeste to use the coach whenever she wanted to escape from the ducal coach and the attached ducal liverymen. It was the carriage they were in today.

She watched the busy hubbub of the city outside the window. It was exciting that she was off to meet Malcolm with her grandfather none the wiser. He would have had a megrim if she'd told him that her maid was pregnant, and she was going to a workshop owned by a bachelor who skated on the outskirts of the *ton* to discuss her maid's future.

"What about the banns?" Celeste turned back to Alice.

Her maid smiled. "Benjamin attends a little church close to his apartments. He's having the first banns called this weekend. I'll attend with him. After three Sundays, we'll marry." Alice glanced at her. "Would you consider...standing with me as a witness?"

Celeste sprang across the carriage, wrapped her arms around Alice, and laughed. "It would be a joy and an honor."

Alice beamed. "Ben is asking Mr. Hollandale to stand with him."

Before Celeste could ask more, the coach slowed to a stop. A coachman opened the door, and Alice stepped out first. Celeste followed but kept her head down. She wore a plain black cloak and a wide-brimmed straw hat, much like horse blinkers. No one needed to know their business. Though they were in a working-class neighborhood, she would not risk being recognized.

As soon as they were at the front door of the workshop, it flew open. Benjamin Brannan stood on the other side with a wide grin and open arms. "My lovely Alice, you're finally here." He swept her into his embrace and twirled her in a circle. Carefully, he set her down with ease. "Come in." Benjamin smiled at Celeste. "You too, Miss Worsley."

Celeste's heartbeat skipped at the glee on Benjamin's face. He and Alice shared the type of love that had the strength to withstand all the asperity and adventures fate could throw in the couple's path. As soon as Alice told Celeste how delighted the young man was at Alice's news, Celeste's belief in love was affirmed.

As tears welled in her eyes, she told herself it was from happiness. She refused to believe she was envious of Alice's good fortune in finding a man who loved her completely. While true love and a happy family were her maid's future, Celeste had a different path in life. That was abiding by her grandfather's wishes so that he'd accept her mother and father into the family and forgive their debt. Her family's future depended on it. If that meant she'd sacrifice her happiness, so be it. She loved her parents and would do anything for them.

As Alice walked hand in hand with Benjamin, Celeste entered. Benjamin took their hats and cloaks.

Malcolm strolled toward them, looking like he'd come directly from his Bond Street tailors. Her breath caught seeing him in a navy silk morning coat, tan breeches, and light blue waistcoat. Whomever his valet was, the man knew how to tie a perfect knot in the neckcloth. Malcolm's boots seemed to shimmer. Proof that his valet must polish them with champagne.

When his gaze met hers, a slow smile spread across his full lips, promising all sorts of wickedness lay in store for her.

If only that were the case. She sighed softly. It wasn't something someone in her position should want, but she craved escaping from her practical but dull pedestal for an hour. Perhaps two hours wouldn't be too greedy. When one was expected to behave as a paragon that people should admire, it was only natural to become a little dizzy at the height of the dais. Who wouldn't want to climb down and live like the rest of the mortals?

Perhaps Malcolm would assist her descent from that pedestal and show her all the things she was missing in life. As she smiled in return, she vowed not to be bothered that he wanted her help finding a wife. Even though she'd repeatedly imagined herself in the role since she'd first seen him, it had only been a fantasy. She knew all too well that he was not the man for her.

"I'll be down in a bit, sir," Benjamin said brightly as he looked at Alice. "My future wife and I need to make plans for the baby."

"Take your time," Malcolm nodded with a grin. "Miss Worsley and I will chat. You can find us in my study."

After the couple took their leave, Celeste awkwardly stood in the entry, waiting for Malcolm to lead the way. He simply stood there staring at her. He seemed as fascinated with her as she was with him.

Which was unusual. For the most part, she blended into the woodwork like a gray mouse in an aged barn. No one really wanted her. A barn cat wouldn't even muster the energy to chase her.

But this gorgeous man looked as if he wished to devour her.

"Is something amiss with my person?" She slid her hand over her midriff to ensure nothing was out of place.

He shook his head as if waking from a dream. "I apologize. It's a rare sight to have a beautiful woman standing in my place of business."

Her cheeks blazed, revealing how his words affected her. She was used to men giving her compliments as bland as a blancmange, but never someone who studied her as if she were one of his experiments. Never known as a missish person except around her grandfather, Celeste tilted her chin and smiled. "And I've never had a handsome man just leave me to stand inside his entry when he invited me to visit."

His look of shock gave way to laughter. "I deserved that. Just punishment, indeed." He waved a hand, signaling her to walk through a bright passageway.

As she walked into the hallway, she stared. Magnificent landscapes and other art hung on the cream-colored silk covering the walls.

"Here's my study." Malcolm opened the door and waved a hand for her to precede him. She bit back a gasp at the opulence of the furnishings inside. The same cream silk covered the study walls. A sitting area consisting of two matching settees in the same silk framed a beautiful marble fireplace. And a massive burled wood desk sat in the center of the room as if reigning over everything in its view. Even the two small chairs in front of the desk perfectly matched the decorations. Black and gray pillows were thrown haphazardly on the various seating surfaces. It was elegant but functional at the same time.

"This is amazing," she murmured.

"I'm glad you like it. I had one of the top designers in London help me craft it to my liking. I find that I prefer simpler designs in my furnishings. My friend, the Duke of Pelham, was the inspiration for this. Robert Adam designed the study, library, and great hall at his ducal seat Pelham Hall." He looked around the room and took a deep breath. "I find I can think clearly here. Nothing is cluttered, including my thoughts." He held out his arm. "Come. There's something else I want to show you."

She slipped her hand around his elbow, and they walked through the room to a side door together. Without hesitating, he threw it open and motioned for her to enter.

After her first step, her breath caught. It was the most feminine study she'd ever seen. Stunning furniture in the Louis XV style surrounded her. A navy desk with gilded feet stood guard over the floor-to-ceiling bookcases painted in a delicate pink with navy accents exactly matched to the desk. Two chaise longues in blue velvet with pink velvet piping were at the room's far end. But the pièce de résistance was a small table with two chairs in a light blue that sat in front of the windows overlooking a small, fenced courtyard. A clock cleverly hidden in the base of a birdcage hung from the ceiling over the table.

"This is like walking into a dream and never wanting to wake up. I could stay here for years and never want to leave. I would only need books, tea, and several biscuits to live a nice life without ever having to deal with the outside world." Celeste twirled slowly as she took in the sight. "What is this place?"

Malcolm rocked back on his heels. "I take it that you approve?"

"Approve? I'm in love with it." She grinned. "I'd like to propose to this room."

He chuckled at her enthusiasm and clasped his hands behind his back as he studied the room with her. "I had it built at the same time as my study. It's my wife's study."

Her heart thudded to a stop. "Your wife?" she asked, hoping her shock wasn't apparent.

"I thought"—he studied the ground for several moments before he grinned at her somewhat sheepishly—"my future wife might want to have a place to work when I worked." He shrugged. "Or a place to read."

Her brow creased as she studied his nervousness. He believed she'd judge him for something so thoughtful. How many men had she met at *ton* events who possessed the foresight to plan a place so he and his spouse could spend more time together?

The answer was not many.

"But I imagine she'd want to redecorate it to her own tastes." His whisky-dark voice dropped, sending goose-bumps up her arms.

She shook her head vehemently. "It's perfect and thoughtful. Your future wife is a lucky...person."

She cleared the sudden lump from her throat. Would the man her grandfather chose as her husband offer the same rare kindness and consideration for her as Malcolm Hollandale had for an unknown woman who was still in his future?

She couldn't allow herself to think such thoughts. Whoever her future husband was, she'd make do. If her grandfather were privy to her fanciful thoughts, he'd criticize her endlessly as being overly sentimental. Affection was not what was important in a marriage. It was a lesson that her mother had forgotten when she ran off to marry the love of her life, Celeste's father.

Her grandfather had always emphasized that it was the connections and the bloodlines each person brought to the marriage that mattered. Grandfather would likely suffer apoplexy if she even suggested marrying someone like Malcolm Hollandale, the son of a country vicar.

"You're very kind." Malcolm turned his sharp gaze to her. "Did I say something wrong?"

Indeed, he had. His concern for a non-existent wife made her feel lonely and a bit frustrated when she thought about her future. The truth was that Malcolm Hollandale was the type of man she'd dreamed of marrying when she was a little girl. A man like her father, who was kind and would love his wife without reservation.

Suddenly, she felt as if she had been sliced open, revealing all her doubts and fears about her future. If she weren't careful, Malcolm Hollandale would see every wound and disappointment she'd ever suffered.

"I'm just a little taken aback by this place. Do you work here?" She took a deep breath and smiled. She had to learn to hide her feelings when she was with him.

"I do. I sometimes sleep here when it's late, and I'm running an experiment." Malcolm strolled to the courtyard windows and pointed to a wing of the building that she hadn't noticed before. "I have a living area for when

I'm unable to break away from my work. I can sleep or rest for a few hours, then return to my laboratory refreshed. I have a cook who comes daily to see to my needs." He pointed to the other wing. "That's where Benjamin lives. I asked for a list of what they'll need to live a comfortable life. It'll be my wedding present to them."

She stood beside him and glanced at the second floor, then turned her gaze to him. "How kind. I haven't even thought about that." She raised her hand to her heart and shook her head. "I never considered what they'd require to care for their baby. What kind of friend am I?"

Perhaps her grandfather's self-centeredness had affected her.

What a horrible thought.

"You're the best kind of friend and employer. You're helping Alice and the baby have the life that they deserve. Good people deserve good things. You deserve those, too."

She hadn't realized she'd said her thoughts loud enough that he could hear them. She nodded slowly, then stepped away. "I'll do more. Alice deserves it." She pulled out a chair from the small table, then regarded Malcolm. "Perhaps we could sit and discuss what requirements you're looking for in a wife?"

He waited until she sat before taking the seat opposite.

"You look like you are sitting at a child's table, ready to play dolls." She tried not to crack a smile.

"What gave it away? The fact that my knees are practically level with my chin?" When they both laughed, he leaned forward with his elbows on the table, then rested his chin in one hand. "That's the first quality."

"What?" she asked as she bit her lip to keep from smiling.

"The ability to laugh." He arched a brow better than

any aristocrat she'd seen before. "My parents always laugh together, and they've been married for over thirty years."

When he wouldn't stop staring at her, she murmured, "I swear there must be something wrong with my face. You keep looking at me."

"You're pretty to look at. That's another requirement for my future wife. She need not be a beauty, but I want to be attracted to her."

"Wait one moment, sir. Was that a compliment?"

He lowered his voice and leaned closer, never taking his gaze from hers. "I said it before. You're stunning and a beauty to look at."

"So, I'd meet that requirement?" Her voice had lowered of its own accord.

"I'm attracted to you. So, what do you think the answer to that is?"

His eyes smoldered with desire. Her heartbeat accelerated, and the blood pounded in her veins. He glanced at the base of her neck.

After a few seconds, he lifted his gaze. Those embers of yearning were still present in the marine-blue of his eyes. "I'd say by the fast rate of your pulse and the look in your eyes that you find me attractive as well."

She swallowed hard, desperate to find the words to deny it but couldn't. She'd never been attracted to a man like she was with him. Even if it were impossible, she'd give him everything if she could. It was a testament to how long she'd wanted him. She couldn't tear her gaze away from his, and he appeared to feel the same.

"Why do you love the theatre? Every time I attend, you're there." He rubbed his thumb along his lower lip. The steady sweep of his thumb made her wish he would touch her that exact same way. She squirmed in her seat as everything inside her grew warm.

"Celeste, answer me," he commanded softly.

She drew in a quivering breath. "Because when I'm there, I can watch the performance and pretend it's me on stage living someone else's life."

"Why would you want another person's life?"

Watching him became almost unbearable. He was hypnotizing her with every movement and every gesture.

"Because my life is not my own. My grandfather will choose whom I marry. That's why I'm helping Alice. I can experience love through her even if I'm only a witness." Her words were like a babbling brook that no one could stop. But it felt so good to confess everything that she was feeling. "You see, I'm a failure in many ways. My grandfather severed all ties with my mother, his only child, because she married my father. I was foolish enough to believe that if he loved me, he'd love my mother. My family lost practically everything in a fire. My father's bank wouldn't loan the money for some reason, so my parents asked my grandfather. Miraculously, he agreed. Several years later, things weren't much better. They couldn't afford a Season for me, so my father asked my grandfather, and once again, he agreed. I want my family to heal their wounds." She shook her head. "I've never told this story to anyone except Alice. Not even my closest friends." Her voice dropped to a whisper. "I'm mortified." Heat crept across her cheeks, but she refused to turn away. "Please don't tell anyone."

"I'm good with secrets." He took her hand and squeezed, the touch intimate and comforting. "You can share anything with me, and I'll keep it safe."

She searched his eyes for pity, but thankfully, there wasn't any. It was the only reason she continued confessing everything she'd locked up for so long.

"Grandfather told me that if I married his choice of

husband, he'd consider reconciling with my mother and forgiving their mortgage. You see, he wants my marriage to be beneficial to him. He said everything about my mother's marriage to my father was a failure to him. *Everything*." She cringed at the words that she'd left unspoken. Her grandfather believed she was a failure since she was a product of their marriage.

"Duchess," he said softly. "You're not a failure. You have to accept that truth for yourself. I'd consider myself the luckiest man in the world if you'd—"

"Well, sir, how else can we help Alice and Ben? That's what I'm here for, correct?" Her voice was a little too bright, and it was the epitome of rudeness to cut him off, but whatever he wanted to ask, she couldn't risk hearing it. If, in the one in a million chance, he had asked her to marry him, she would probably blurt out a "yes."

In response, he kissed her hand. The tenderness of his expression and the single kiss almost undid her. Tears swelled but she blinked, refusing to let them fall. Her destiny was in the control of her grandfather. "Don't, please. I can't bear it." She shut her eyes. "I've always wanted a man like you, but you're entirely wrong for me."

Still holding her hand, he leaned slightly away. "How am I wrong for you?"

"Please don't misconstrue my meaning." This time she was the one to offer comfort by squeezing his hand. "It would be like wanting to eat an entire cake in one sitting. It would taste so good, but I'd be sick afterward."

He searched her eyes, as if trying to understand.

His bewilderment matched her own. How to explain that she couldn't forsake her parents for her own benefit? It would be her wildest dream to be married to a man like Malcolm Hollandale, but the aftermath with her grandfather would be too much to bear.

"I can assure you that with me, you can have all the cake you want. I'll keep you in perfect health," he whispered as he lowered his face to hers.

Slowly, she closed her eyes. He was going to kiss her, and she wanted it more than anything she'd ever desired in her life.

Suddenly, an unmitigated, muffled yowl echoed behind a door.

He pulled away as he murmured, "Damnation."

Answering his curse, a chorus of yowls and meows joined the first intruder who interrupted them.

"What is that?" she asked cautiously as she regarded him. He didn't seem too pleased with whatever made those indescribable sounds.

"Kittens." He rested his forehead in his hands. "Those ungrateful, swarming felines."

Then, an ungodly caterwaul erupted.

"And that?" Celeste looked toward the door. If she wasn't mistaken, Malcolm growled when she pulled away.

"Their mother," he groaned. "She must be hungry."

"You have kittens? Oh, my goodness. *You have kittens*." Her smile grew wider than the Thames as she waggled her eyebrows. "I love kittens."

He stood and held out his hand. "Shall we find the little beasties and see what they want?"

His eyes flashed with pleasure as she took his hand. "Yes, please. Let's not keep them waiting."

"I warn you." One side of his mouth tugged into a grin worthy of a rogue. "These kittens are not for the faint of heart."

"Neither are you," she murmured.

CHAPTER FOUR

As soon as Malcolm opened the door, the kittens tumbled forward like a clumsy marauding band of pirates. En masse, they started, or at least attempted, to climb his boots. Much to his amazement, Celeste fell into a heap on the floor, her skirts *swooshing* around her. She cooed and cuddled with the irritating balls of fluff. Their calico mother sauntered into the room with her tail raised in a straight line. The smug look on her face undoubtedly meant *feed me, fool. Please don't make me meow it twice.*

"Oh, you are darling," Celeste soothed as she picked up the one with long, fluffy white fur. The kitten proceeded to claw her way up Celeste's dress.

He walked to a side table and picked up a bowl. The mother cat raced to his side and rubbed against his leg until he set the food down. Dismissing him, she turned her attention to the scraps of meat and daintily ate one morsel at a time.

"Tired of them already?" Malcolm petted her as he glanced at Celeste. "She seems enchanted with your brood," he murmured to his cat. "I almost kissed her, but your ruffians barged in. This might work even better. I'll charm her with kittens. Good thinking on your part that you wanted to eat. Extra helpings for you tonight."

Sitting on the floor, Celeste looked up at him. "Did you say something?"

"Nothing worth sharing," he answered.

In that moment, he wished for time to stand still. Her eyes sparkled with adoration and happiness. He'd always imagined his wife would accompany him to his workplace and spend the day doing whatever she wanted—working, reading, writing, whatever brought her pleasure. Then, he'd come and see her when he took a much-needed break, and she would do the same. Being here with Celeste was precisely how he'd pictured life with a wife.

Good heavens, he'd almost kissed her earlier and practically told her she was the ideal woman to be his wife. He blew out a breath as he ran a hand through his hair.

Malcolm considered himself a realist. Of all the ladies of the *ton*, Celeste Worsley was the one he'd be least likely to marry-*even if she almost allowed him to kiss her.* Her grandfather would never approve of him.

He dismissed the devilish voice that suggested she was attracted to him as much as he was to her. Celeste had confessed she saw herself as the epitome of a dutiful society miss. She'd already agreed to marry the man her grandfather, one of Britain's wealthiest and most powerful men, would choose for her. Mayhap, Celeste didn't have the option to defy him.

He couldn't quit staring at her. She was like a piece of art that a person didn't care for at first. But if you studied it, you'd come to appreciate every stroke of the brush that made the entire work magnificent.

"Malcolm, what are their names?" His gut clenched at the lyrical sound of his name in her honeyed voice. It was a reminder of the danger that existed if he became too close to her.

"One." He pointed to the white kitten. "Two." He scooped the black kitten with white socks into his arms and brought it to his chest. The kitten proceeded to bat at his nose with one white paw. "Three." He pointed to a gray tiger-striped kitten who struggled but jumped onto her lap.

"Seriously?" Her lush pink lips scrounged into a frown. "That's what you named them?"

"Well, Mrs. Cat was delivering her kittens so fast, I couldn't spend the time to name them based upon their personality. I could have named them first, second, third—"

"Enough," she said with a rueful chuckle.

He picked up a black cat with beautiful green eyes. "This handsome fellow—"

"Let me guess," she said, shaking her head with a smile. "Four."

"Actually, he's Five." Malcolm glanced around and found the tiny calico kitten, the spitting image of her mother. "This is Four."

Celeste brought the white kitten to her face and rubbed her cheek against its soft fur. "I always wanted a kitten."

"Why didn't you have one?" He sat cross-legged across from her. All the kittens scampered toward him and proceeded to climb into his lap.

Celeste caught Two with her free hand and brought him to her chest.

Lucky devil.

"My parents allowed me to have pets, but they were dogs. Never a cat. My father always sneezes around the barn cats. When I asked for a pet in London, my grandfather wouldn't allow it." When Two struggled to get down, she set him on Malcolm's lap.

He hissed softly at the brush of her hand on his leg, then grabbed it before she could pull away. "Your grandfather wouldn't let you bring your pets?"

"Pfft." She laughed as he entwined their fingers together. "I didn't have any when I came to London, but I wanted one. When I asked, he told me a dog's only purpose was to turn the spit in the kitchen or retrieve waterfowl that he'd shot." She rolled her eyes. "Cats are good for being mousers and are only allowed in the kitchen and the barn."

While she tried to make light of her grandfather, he could tell by the longing in her eyes that it was more than not being allowed to have a pet. He leaned close and studied their hands before capturing her gaze. "If I'd known you when you were a little girl, I would have snuck a kitten into your room. You obviously adore them."

By the massive smile on her face, he'd said the right thing.

She kissed One on its head, then smiled shyly at him. "I would have liked to have known you when you were a lad. I imagine there was never a dull moment. Where did you grow up?"

"Wiltshire. My father was the local vicar in a small village. He supplemented his income by tutoring several young lords and a few sons of the wealthy local gentry. One of the fathers was so impressed by my father's ability to teach his son that he sponsored me at Eton and then paid my Oxford tuition. One of the boys he tutored became the Duke of Pelham. At Eton, I met the Marquess of Ravenscroft and the Earl of Trafford. We've been friends ever since."

"When did you become a member of Pelham's Millionaires Club?"

He eyed her to see if anything was conniving about her

questions. Most women wanted to know the amount of money in his bank before they deemed him worthy of their attention. But Celeste was utterly bewitched by the kittens and wasn't even looking at him.

"I assume you are asking me about my work," he said innocently.

"Yes," she murmured, then played with a ribbon that enchanted One. "What do you do all day?"

He relaxed. She didn't care about his wealth. She was completely different from other women. Perhaps his first impression of her was wrong. She was simply curious about *him*.

"I have a laboratory downstairs. I make glazes for ceramics, china, and the like. I'm working on several formulas for making glazes and varnishes for wood floors, so the wood is preserved."

She smiled at him innocently. "So, you're a chemist."

He nodded, pleased with her assumption. Most people thought him a laborer at best, but Malcolm had taken first in science, chemistry, mathematics, and physics at university. He had a natural affinity for the sciences and loved his work.

"That's impressive." Celeste tilted her head. "I'm a little surprised you have a cat as a pet."

"Everyone needs friends, and they make great companions." He nodded toward Mrs. Cat. "She listens while I muse on why something I'm creating doesn't work."

"Does Mrs. Cat give you advice?" Celeste grinned.

He shook his head as he chuckled. "No. She normally yawns, letting me know how boring I am, then strolls from the room looking for entertainment."

"Well, if it's any consolation, I don't think you're boring." She smiled mischievously. "However, I'm not as discriminating as your Mrs. Cat."

They both turned to watch the mother cat, who had finished her meal and then had one back leg stretched toward the ceiling and proceeded to clean herself. The cat stopped for a second and regarded Malcolm. With a dismissive blink, she went back to her ablutions.

"I think you're fascinating. Mrs. Cat has no idea how lucky she is to have you."

He tried to smile, but damnation, all he wanted to do was haul her against him and kiss her. She wasn't condescending. She fancied him. Just as he fancied her.

The hell with it.

Without hesitating, he closed the distance between them and pressed his lips to hers. Her eyes fluttered once, twice, then closed. She leaned near and rested her hand on his chest, the touch so endearing that he couldn't help himself from cupping her cheeks and deepening the kiss.

Gently, so as not to scare her, Malcolm traced the seam of her lips with his tongue, begging her to let him taste more of her sweetness. She stiffened slightly, then with a sigh, she opened for him. He slid his tongue against hers and groaned. She tasted like heaven and sin wrapped together and tied with a bow. He took his time and savored her as he explored every inch of her mouth.

Then, the clever and resourceful woman twisted the tables on him. When he took a breath, she slipped her tongue into his mouth. The escaped moan was so erotic that he pulled her tighter against him. Her tongue twisted with his as if they had done this a thousand times before.

He couldn't get enough of her taste, her smell, or the feel of her soft skin against his. He feared that he'd never get enough of her.

"Malcolm," she whispered.

His name on her lips lit a fire inside of him, driving him wild. With his mouth and tongue, Malcolm tasted the sweet skin of her throat until he reached the pounding pulse at the base of her neck. He felt the same.

When he tried to pull her onto his lap, she resisted but tilted her head back so he could caress the tender skin of her neck. "Watch for the kittens."

"They're fine," he assured her.

But the kittens had different opinions. One meowed in distress, and Celeste broke their kiss to see who fretted. She quickly pulled her favorite white furball toward her chest, then buried her face against it.

His mind counseled that he was getting too close, but his body argued that kissing her was the most natural thing in the world. His heartbeat slowed as he gently skated his hands up and down her back in a comforting rhythm.

"Too much?" he asked gently.

"I think the sooner we can find you a wife, the better," she murmured as she set One down. The kitten instantly started to climb Malcolm's lap.

He felt lower than a toadstool. "I apologize."

"Don't," she whispered.

The little beast batted at one of the buttons of his waistcoat but missed. Instead, one of its sharp but tiny claws caught on the fine silk and pulled it.

"Oh no, darling," she crooned as she untangled its claw from the material and brought the kitten close. "Are you hurt?" She rubbed her cheek against its soft fur.

"If you're asking me, the answer is no." He raised an eyebrow. "But it wounds me to think you're more worried about One than me."

She leaned back and smiled his way. The way her eyes were lowered, and the pull of her lips made her appear drunk. It was an intoxicating look on her. He wanted to pound his chest at the expression. He'd caused that. It took every ounce of restraint not to take her in another scorching kiss.

"You were saying something about a wife? Are you applying for the position?" He'd heard every word she'd uttered, but the devil inside of him wanted to hear her say that she didn't want him. She wouldn't be the first. Even if she said she wasn't for him, Malcolm would have difficulty believing it based on how she'd kissed him as if her next breath depended on it.

Her cheeks heated, but Celeste held his gaze. "I wouldn't make you a good wife. I'd disappoint you."

Of all the excuses she could have used, that was the last thing he had expected. "Why would you think that?"

"I disappoint everyone. Everyone in my family is a disappointment according to my grandfather." She pressed a kiss to the kitten's head, then petted the rest of them before she stood and brushed her skirts. "I must find Alice, and then we should leave."

He stood as well. "So soon?"

She nodded. "Will you be at the Ravenscroft ball this week?"

"Yes." He escorted her to the door.

"I'll see you then." Celeste turned back and smiled fondly at the kittens one last time. "Thank you for sharing them with me. I don't recall ever having such fun." Another beautiful blush colored her cheeks. "I enjoyed our time together."

"As did I," Malcolm murmured. "Especially the kiss."

Then and there, he decided he was giving her the white kitten when it was weaned, even if he had to hire a servant to take care of the little beastie for her.

She reached for the door latch.

"Duchess?" When she turned to face him, he took her hand and raised it to his lips. "You'd never disappoint me."

She tried to smile as her eyes glistened with tears, but she didn't answer him. Instead, she turned on one heel and left the room.

They were playing an incendiary game, and he wondered if either of them understood the rules. It wasn't like a controlled experiments in his laboratory. There he knew how to manipulate the compounds for the desired result. Whatever it was between him and Celeste threatened to combust into flames. He'd never felt so alive. For once in his life, he wanted to pursue what was between them, no matter how reckless. Celeste Worsley was a woman who didn't think him beneath her. He ran his hand through his hair.

He was probably being naïve, but he didn't think he'd be burned.

The next day, Malcolm entered the Duke of Pelham's study.

"Well, well, well," Dane Ardeerton, the Duke of Pelham, slowly rose from his desk and examined Malcolm from head to foot. "If it isn't my favorite inventor."

"I prefer chemist," Malcolm retorted with a laugh as he entered the duke's study.

"I'll call you anything you'd like, including darling, if you continue to make me money."

The duke waved him forward in welcome. Exceedingly tall with brilliant blue eyes, blond hair that could be mistaken for spun gold, and looks that Apollo would be jealous of, Pelham was a sight to behold. No wonder all the ladies of the *ton* had set their caps for him. As the owner of the Jolly Rooster, a gambling hell next to his ducal estate disguised as a coaching inn, Pelham loved to make money. He was so successful at it that he was one of the rare millionaires in the British Isles. He'd even created an exclusive club called the Millionaires of Mayfair to help other millionaires protect and grow their fortunes.

Pelham was an astute problem solver and an expert on human nature. It was why he was so successful at gambling. Malcolm always sought advice when he was troubled. The only way he knew how to secure Celeste's hand was by impressing her grandfather. To do that, he needed Pelham's help.

"Hollandale," Marcus Kirkland, the Earl of Trafford, called out. "Come in and save us from Pelham's latest outrageous idea for making money." Trafford had taken Malcolm under his wing when Malcolm had first set foot into Eton. Whenever Trafford was near, the other students never dared snub Malcolm. Trafford had become one of his closest friends because of it.

Hugh Calthorp, the Marquess of Ravenscroft, rose from his chair and was the first to extend his hand to Malcolm. "Good to see you, old man. Are you coming to my mother's ball?"

The jovial marquess stood taller than Malcolm by an inch. With hair the color of a raven's wings and mischievous eyes, Ravenscroft was loyal and a true friend to Malcolm. But his most endearing trait was that he never allowed anyone to take themselves too seriously.

"I wouldn't miss it for anything." Malcolm shook his friend's hand.

"What about one of my masquerades?" Pelham lifted an aristocratic eyebrow.

"I've become fond of them ever since I attended the last one," Trafford said with a grin, then shook Malcolm's hand.

"Let me explain Pelham's obsession with masquerades, Hollandale," Ravenscroft said as he eyed the duke with a smile. "He gets to dress like a Greek god, women vie for his attention, and his friends are especially generous in contributing their allowances and hard-earned money to his games of chance."

"Even you must admit I'm still handsome, debonair, and suave even while wearing a sheet tied around my waist." Pelham tilted his chin in the air as only he could do.

Malcolm always felt welcome in their presence, no matter the chaffing that occurred between them.

"Hollandale, you should come to the next party I host," Pelham announced.

Malcolm shook his head. "Every time you ask me, you know my answer."

Ravenscroft tilted his face to the ceiling and roared with laughter. Trafford joined in.

"What?" Pelham asked with a feigned hint of offense.

"Why do you do this to yourself? Hollandale will say no, just as he has the last one hundred and one times before that." Ravenscroft wiped his eyes.

"Well," Pelham huffed. "I don't want the man to feel left out."

"Thank you, my friend." Malcolm grinned.

The duke surprised him by lightly slapping his back. "I'm well aware that games of chance aren't your favorite pastime, but I'd like your company. My French chef is the best in all of England. Napoleon even tried to hire him out from underneath my nose." The duke huffed a disgruntled curse. "And as importantly, it's beautiful there, and you're always welcome to stay at Pelham Hall."

"And at my estate," Ravenscroft offered.

"Mine too," Trafford said with a smile.

Malcolm nodded, unable to speak since his throat had tightened with emotion. Three of the country's most influential and wealthy peers always treated him as an equal. Their friendship was one of the most valuable things he possessed. He was awed whenever he spent time with them, especially Pelham.

Pelham waved toward the last empty chair around his burled wood desk. He poured a whisky and set it in front of the chair. "Sit down and tell us what brings you here. Another new varnish or glaze for me to see? I should visit your laboratory this week."

Malcolm nodded. "You're always welcome. But that's not why I'm here." He sipped from the tumbler, then leaned forward, resting his elbows on his thighs. He dangled the glass from one of his hands. "I've come for information."

Trafford waggled his eyebrows. "Then you're in the right place. Pelham knows all."

"Well, almost all," Ravenscroft said as he winked.

Trafford suddenly became interested in his glass of whisky. Pelham pursed his lips in aggravation. It was a sign not to broach whatever Ravenscroft was inferring.

Malcolm glanced at the three friends. Something was afoot, but they would tell him in due time. They always did without him having to pry. But if Malcolm were a betting man, he'd lay ten-to-one odds it had something to do with one of Pelham's sisters.

He finished his whisky and set the empty glass on the side table next to him. "What do you know about the Duke of Exehill."

Pelham remained immobile. Trafford and Ravenscroft sat up a bit taller at the mention of the duke's name.

"What would you like to know?" Pelham asked nonchalantly.

Malcolm exhaled as he debated how much to share. He was closer to these men than anyone else in his life. If he couldn't trust them, then he couldn't trust anyone.

"I had the most unusual exchange with his grand-daughter, Miss Celeste Worsley. She approached me at the theatre where I was working and asked to chat privately."

"Celeste Worsley?" Ravenscroft asked. By his eager posture, he couldn't wait to hear the details of Malcolm's story.

Malcolm nodded. "She needed help from me with a personal matter, and in exchange, she said she'd help me find a suitable wife."

Trafford rubbed his hands together. "I can't wait to hear this."

"Don't you call her duchess of something?" Ravenscroft asked.

"The Duchess of Drury Lane," Malcolm admitted sheepishly. "She's always at the theatre. When she and I make eye contact, she looks down her nose at me...or at least, she did."

"And what has changed?" Pelham arched a perfect aristocratic eyebrow as only a duke could do.

"Since perhaps I kissed her," Malcolm murmured.

"And when did that occur? Doubtful Exehill was near." Ravenscroft's voice deepened with a hint of intrigue.

"I'll get to that," Malcolm waved a hand. "Her lady's maid, Alice Cummings, is pregnant by one of my employees. Celeste wants me to hire her as a servant in my home so she can marry my employee. She's convinced that if her grandfather finds out, he'll dismiss the maid without references or her wages. Celeste has offered to pay the maid's wages."

"What?" Trafford said incredulously. "Are you serious? What will you do with a lady's maid?"

"Nothing but give her and Benjamin shelter. Benjamin lives above my laboratory. He and Alice can live there." Malcolm leaned back against the chair.

Pelham regarded him with narrowed eyes. "I can believe Exehill would do such a thing to his granddaughter. He broke all ties with his only child, Lady Susan, when she married Lord Worsley. Exehill has refused to acknowledge his daughter since her wedding."

Malcolm thrummed his fingers against the arm of the chair. Everything that Celeste had said was true. But then, he'd never really doubted her, not when her green eyes had filled with worry when she'd explained the situation about Alice.

"Why did she come to you? Why not go to your employee?" Trafford asked.

"Good question. I think it's because she trusts me." Without second-guessing himself, Malcolm continued, "Apparently, Celeste's grandfather is expected to make a match for her with a man he deems be suitable."

He dismissed his trepidation. Logically, he surmised that the duke could accept him as a suitable candidate for his granddaughter's hand. He was wealthy, lived in Mayfair a few streets from the duke, and considered himself honorable. He'd make Celeste happy and give her anything she wanted. Malcolm simply had to find a way to convince the duke of that.

Pelham's gaze was still locked on Malcolm. "You care for the girl?"

At the sudden quiet, he could have heard a feather drop in the room.

Malcolm nodded. "She said if I helped her with her maid, she'd help me find a wife." He glanced at each man in turn. "I want her."

"I thought you didn't care for her?" Pelham scowled.

"I didn't know her. Even if she weren't part of the *ton*, I'd want her."

"Really?" Trafford asked. "I thought that was one of your requirements."

He'd thought so too. But being an outsider didn't matter when he was with her. "Not anymore."

Ravenscroft blew out a breath. "Good for you, old man. Celeste Worsley would be fortunate to have you as her husband. And the same for you."

"Hear, hear," Trafford called out.

"It's not that easy." Malcolm held up his hand. "Celeste believes that she can mend the rift between her parents and the duke by marrying the man her grandfather chooses for her. He'll also forgive a mortgage he holds on her father's estate."

Ravenscroft tipped his head toward the ceiling and tapped one cheek with a finger. "It's all coming back to me now. My mother attended a party when Exehill delivered a cut direct to his own daughter and her husband. They eloped to Scotland several weeks before without the duke's consent. Rumor had it that he wanted his daughter to marry a peer he'd chosen. I can't remember the name."

"I gather that you would like to be the man that Exehill chooses for his granddaughter?" Pelham asked in a deceptive yet leisurely voice. It was the one he always used when he was plotting something.

"Yes," Malcolm said without hesitation.

"Have you made Exehill's acquaintance?" Pelham arched a brow.

Malcolm shook his head. "I was hoping—"

"That I would host a dinner party?" Pelham slammed his hand on the wooden surface of his desk. "*Brilliant*. My sisters are in town for the Season. Honoria and Pippa have been after me to invite guests to Ardeerton Hall. This will be perfect." He nodded as if the decision was final. "When do you want to have it?"

Malcolm shook his head silently at the speed at which Pelham decided. "Wouldn't you like to ask your sisters if they wish to host such an event?"

"They'll be ecstatic," Pelham said with a dismissive wave of his hand. "I'll have the *Governess* help them host it. She's a dear friend of Pippa's and a new friend to Honoria. The *Governess* is helping smooth Honoria's entrance into society."

Ravenscroft coughed into his closed fist, but there was laughter in his eyes.

"Pelham," Trafford warned. "I don't believe your eldest sister Honoria cares for such activities."

Pelham stood from his desk and glared at Trafford.

Trafford did the same. After a few tense moments, both men relaxed.

"How fortunate the *Governess* is here." Ravenscroft chuckled.

Pelham's nostrils flared in rebuke for the marquess's joke.

Malcolm watched the drama that was unfolding before him.

The *Governess*, Lady Grace Webster, was an exemplary member of the *ton* and used her status to help other members who unfortunately found themselves dancing with scandal. Because of her prowess and ability to lead her so-called charges through the dangerous nuances of *ton* life with their reputations intact, she was referred to as the *Governess*.

There had been a vague reference or two when they'd left university that Pelham had set his mind on a match with Grace. But as with most rumors, very little of it had any truth. So, the idea that Lady Honoria needed Lady

Grace's assistance meant there was more to her presence in London than just presenting her to society. Nevertheless, it would not be a subject that Malcolm would pursue. The Duke of Pelham was more protective of his sisters than a wet hen with her chicks. He would never allow any rumors to run amok about either of his sisters.

The duke turned his attention to Malcolm. "I'll have Exehill and his granddaughter here. Dress in your finest. I'll be singing your praises." He gazed over to Trafford and Ravenscroft. "I expect you to do the same."

"Of course," Ravenscroft chortled. "As long as it's Hollandale getting married and not me."

Pelham cracked a smile, but Trafford just glowered at his two friends.

"I can't thank you enough," Malcolm stood and took his leave.

As he exited Ardeerton House, Malcolm's step was a little lighter. He didn't want just any woman as his wife. He wanted his duchess. And if he did play one of Pelham's games of chance, he'd say that the odds were in his favor that he would be proposing to Miss Celeste Worsley in the not-too-distant future.

CHAPTER FIVE

With an elegance only a duke could possess, Celeste's grandfather smoothed the serviette in his lap. With a slight smile, Theodore Herbert Grandon, the Seventh Duke of Exehill, looked every bit the part of a haughty aristocrat. With his aquiline nose, sharp cheekbones, and steely blue eyes, all framed by a thick, snowy white head of hair, he was still as imposing as the first time she'd met him eight years ago when she'd been thirteen years of age.

He snapped his fingers, and immediately, a footman, dressed in the gold and ivory livery with gold buttons bearing the ducal crest, offered him a plate of kippers. The duke nodded once, and the footman served him.

The footman's deferential attendance on the duke reminded her of how quickly she'd come when he'd called for her to visit him in London. With a snap of her grandfather's fingers, she'd left home to see him for the first time. She'd stayed two weeks.

The experience was so different from how she'd been raised. In her home, her mother helped the cook in the kitchen, and her father worked in his stables and the fields, lending assistance wherever an extra hand was needed.

Her grandfather would have been appalled at how his daughter and granddaughter lived, but Celeste loved it. She'd been raised with love and tenderness. Her parents had agreed for her to visit her grandfather during the Season. Since they didn't have the funds to dress Celeste in silk gowns, morning dresses for social calls, ball gowns, matching gloves and shoes, and other accompaniments, they'd asked her grandfather. Surprisingly, he'd agreed.

He'd been delighted when she'd arrived and had charmed her with little effort. She couldn't say she adored her grandfather, but she did respect him... except when he became upset with his servants. And she didn't care for it when he started to discuss possible marital prospects.

"My dear, how did you enjoy the Hartfords' soiree last week?" her grandfather asked while cutting a piece of ham. He studied her with *that look* as he placed a bit in his mouth.

That look referred to how he would evaluate Celeste as if she were a prime piece of horseflesh about to go up on the auction block. Frankly, how he looked her over gave her chills. But he'd been forthcoming ever since she'd arrived in London. *People of our ilk don't marry for love. We marry for family dynasties which helped protect and foster the family fortunes.* Even though her grandfather didn't have an heir, he always pontificated that it was his highest duty to leave the duchy wealthier than when he'd inherited it. Celeste was essential to that endeavor.

And she had to remember that she'd accepted that fate. Her grandfather had squired her to *ton* events and bought her a fortune in clothing. Not that she was trying to repay him, but she knew her part in this particular play.

Celeste daintily pressed her serviette to the corners of

her mouth, then placed it in her lap before she spoke a word. Her deportment lesson instructor had insisted that a ducal granddaughter must follow the same etiquette rules as a ducal daughter. Though Celeste hated it, knowing her mother had to follow these same customs when she grew up made the task somewhat easier.

"I enjoyed the Hartfords' event immensely. Many of my friends from finishing school were there. Lady Amelia and Lady Pippa attended." When he smiled his approval, she answered in kind.

"Lady Pippa is a fine person to emulate," her grandfather lectured. "Her manners are impeccable, and she always wears understated but intriguing gowns. Though her brother, the Duke of Pelham, is one of the wealthiest in the country, she doesn't flaunt her wealth by wearing jewels or silly fashions.

"I heartily agree." Celeste bit her lip to stifle the laugh that bubbled in her chest. Everyone knew that Lady Pippa was beautiful but eccentric. She wanted nothing more than to purchase a modiste shop and create gowns. In essence, a ducal sister wanted to be in trade. Her grandfather would suffer from an apoplexy if he knew the truth about Pippa.

"I'd consider the Duke of Pelham a worthy suitor if he didn't own that gambling hell next to his ducal estate, Pelham Hall." Her grandfather shook his head and pushed away his plate, signaling that he had finished his meal but wanted another cup of tea. As the footman cleared his plate, another filled his cup. "In my estimation, it's a bit gauche for a duke to exhibit such behavior."

Celeste kept her hands in her lap and her gaze glued to her plate. The Duke of Pelham was gorgeous. He was one of the most handsome men she'd ever laid eyes on, with the exception of Malcolm Hollandale. But the duke wasn't for her. He had no interest in marriage. At least, that's what everyone had gossiped about since she'd been in London. Practically every eligible young lady wanted the duke as a husband. His wealth, looks, and devil-may-care attitude made a girl turn her head twice, if not thrice, when he passed by.

Her grandfather patted a bony hand on her arm. "Not to worry, my dear. I'm on the hunt for the perfect husband for you. A man of honor who understands the duty to his title will be the person who will be worthy of your hand."

"That means you will invite Mother and Father to town?" She swallowed slightly, hoping he didn't see her nervousness whenever she brought up her parents. But she'd agreed to his plan when she'd first arrived in town as long as her parents were part of the announcement.

He leaned back against his chair and examined her like she was a day-old fish at a fishmonger's stall at the market. The quirk of his eyebrow betrayed his exasperation at her question. "I've promised you that."

She smiled in gratitude.

"But we shall see if they want to come. I've made it clear what I've thought of their marriage." He shook his head. "Pfft."

Celeste breathed deeply in preparation for the diatribe that would erupt from his mouth. He would regale her with every sin that her mother and father had committed when they'd fallen in love.

"Disgraceful and unnecessary. Married by special license indeed." He wagged his finger at her. "Six months later, you were born. The midwife informed me that you were born too early. However, you were a healthy size baby."

Celeste closed her eyes. Her grandfather had sent a midwife to evaluate her mother and her health, one of the rare signs that he cared about his only child. The midwife was shocked to see that her mother had already delivered Celeste.

He shook his head. Thankfully, whatever rampage brewed in his mind, he conquered it.

"I'm having luncheon with the Marquess of Grolier tomorrow. Don't forget that we shall attend the Marquess of Ravenscroft's ball. Later in the week, we shall attend a dinner party given by the Duke of Pelham and his sisters. The Marquess of Ravenscroft and the Earl of Trafford will be there. Fine men, but their titles aren't worthy enough to marry the Duke of Exehill's granddaughter," he declared as he pointed his finger skyward as if he were Moses delivering the ten commandments. "The following week, a new play will premiere at the Theatre Royal, Drury Lane." His brow furrowed. "I can't remember the title."

"It's Lady of the Scullery. The playwright is Lady Giselle." When her grandfather scowled, Celeste smiled. "You must remember that her father is a duke. The Prince Regent is quite an admirer of her work."

Celeste had no idea if that was true, but the theatre was her love. She could admire the costumes and the sets, and the stories kept her enthralled. It made no difference if they were comedies or tragedies. Before the plays started, one of her favorite things to do was study the assembled crowd. She'd find couples sitting together, then imagine their love stories.

Yet her favorite thing was to watch Malcolm. It was the perfect opportunity to watch the man to her heart's content without being caught. His box was next to her grandfather's, allowing an unobstructed view of him.

"Well, if it's good enough for the Prince Regent, then it will have to do." Her grandfather waved his hand. Immediately, the two footmen serving them left the small breakfast room. As soon as the doors shut behind them, her grandfather leaned back in his chair and stared at her. "Your lady's maid? What is her name?"

"Alice Cummings." Celeste didn't blink as an anxious swarm of butterflies fluttered in her chest. She tightly clutched her hands under the table and smiled. "Is something amiss?"

"I don't know," her grandfather answered. "Mrs. Portland came to see me."

Celeste didn't twitch as anger replaced anxiety. Her grandfather's housekeeper was notorious for snitching on the staff. Celeste had informed Alice to stay far away from that woman if at all possible.

"A matter of grave urgency has been brought to my attention. Your lady's maid has been ill in the mornings. Mrs. Portland believes the girl has gained weight over the last several months." Her grandfather narrowed his eyes. "Do you know anything about her health?"

"She's perfectly fine," The words erupted from Celeste's mouth a little too fervently and a tad quarrelsome. "Sometimes I ask her to sit with me in the mornings when I have a cup of tea and share a tart or two."

Her grandfather thrummed his fingers on the table as he nodded. "I see. It would be best if you didn't become too friendly with the staff. It isn't healthy for a young woman such as you."

It took every ounce of restraint she had not to roll her eyes. But somehow, she managed it. "I'll cease asking her to keep me company."

"I don't mean to be indelicate, but you were raised on a farm," he mused, then trained his gaze to hers. "Mrs. Portland suspects Alice might be carrying." Her grandfather narrowed his eyes. "What do you think?"

"I don't know." Celeste forced her gaze to his. "I'll speak to her about it."

"That won't be necessary. I'll have Mrs. Portland do it." He stood slowly, and Celeste followed. "Perhaps you should start interviewing for another lady's maid."

And there it was. The confirmation that she dreaded. He would fire Alice before the day was over.

"What are your plans for the day?" he asked.

"A little shopping is all," Celeste said. He never wanted to accompany her when she did that, and Celeste could stay out as long as she wanted. It would give her time to gather Alice and take her to Benjamin's rooms above Malcolm's laboratory.

"Take another maid to accompany you. I don't want you to be seen with Alice anymore." He turned to walk out the door.

Celeste fisted her hands. It wasn't that Alice didn't have a place to stay. Of course, she could stay with Benjamin. But Alice deserved better treatment than being fired by her grandfather. If they let her go today, Celeste doubted Mrs. Portland would pay her the wages she was owed.

"Your Grace?" When her grandfather turned around, Celeste smiled. "Alice is a wonderful lady's maid. There's no one more talented than her. Please don't let her go."

"I don't allow immoral people to live in my home. No matter their station in life," he said But his eyes flashed with barely disguised anger. "That includes your mother."

"They were in love." Celeste's hand flew to her mouth. She'd never been this belligerent with her grandfather before.

He narrowed his eyes as he regarded her. "That's not an excuse for what your father did to me."

"What did he do to you?" Celeste's voice had grown weak. She hated to sound timid, but she'd seen her grandfather's anger take flight when he'd met with his solicitor.

He could tear a person apart with his barbed tongue in minutes.

"He turned your mother into a whore. He destroyed my only daughter, my flesh and blood." Her grandfather clasped his hands behind his back and regarded her.

Celeste remained frozen as her grandfather's words echoed around her. He considered her beautiful and kind mother as someone who didn't deserve his affection or attention because she'd fallen in love with Celeste's father.

Her stomach roiled at his bitter words. It hurt worse than a slap in the face. If he thought her mother was a whore, there was no telling what he would do to Alice.

"Regarding your lady's maid, Mrs. Portland advised me that the teaspoon silver set your grandmother received from the queen is missing. She also made mention that Alice was seen leaving one evening with a bag that 'rattled.' She needs money for the babe, I assume." Without another word, her grandfather strolled out of the room with his head held high.

He could have Alice transported to another country for theft, and Celeste wouldn't be able to defend her. Her grandfather had friends in high places who would kidnap Alice in the dead of night without Celeste even suspecting anything was amiss. Alice would be all alone with the baby without any food, clothing, or money.

There was no time to delay. She had to help Alice collect her belongings. She couldn't stay another night here.

Which meant Celeste had to see Malcolm immediately.

Not expecting any visitors this early in the morning, Malcolm grunted with annoyance at the knock at the door. He was in the middle of an experiment for a new wood varnishing formula. Opening night was less than two weeks away, and he wanted the stage at Drury Lane to shine.

As soon as he answered the door, his impatience evaporated like rain on a hot July day.

Alone, Celeste stood on his doorstep with a wide-brimmed hat clutching her reticule like a buoy in rough seas. "May I come in?"

"Of course," he said as he motioned her inside. He stole a quick peek over her shoulder. No carriage waited for her, and Alice was nowhere in sight. "Where is your lady's maid?"

"I sent her to the market. Afterward, she's to come here. Is Benjamin here?" Celeste untied the ribbon under her chin and took off the hat.

"He's downstairs in the laboratory."

She cast a furtive glance toward the downstairs steps, then stepped a little closer. "May we go someplace private?"

"What's happened?"

She was frightened out of her mind. Gone was the delightful pink in her cheeks as she worried her bottom lip with her teeth. Without hesitating, Malcolm took her in his arms. Instantly, she buried her head against his chest. He inhaled the sweet scent of roses that followed her wherever she went. For the love of heaven, she fit perfectly in his arms. As he held her, an overwhelming need to right anything amiss in her world took hold of him. "Whatever it is, I'll fix it."

She pulled away, and he resisted the urge to haul her back into his arms.

"I don't know if you can. It's my grandfather." She brought her reticule close to her chest as if using the small bag as a shield.

He took her hand and gently pulled her toward his study. "Come."

She squeezed his hand and followed without another word. As soon as they entered, Malcolm closed the door behind them.

He didn't release her hand as he led her to the sitting area that overlooked the small courtyard. As soon as she perched on the edge of one of the chairs, he angled his body to see her expression.

She was terrified.

"Thank you for seeing me under such circumstances."

He smiled. "I would see you *under or over* any circumstance."

The delightful pink returned to her cheeks. It was quickly becoming his favorite color.

"Thank you."

He leaned close enough to see the swirls of gold that made her green eyes shimmer in the light. He'd never tire of such a sight and instantly wondered if her eyes would glimmer with that color when she was in the throes of passion. It was a wicked idea, but he couldn't erase it from his thoughts. Every time he saw her, his attraction grew.

"I don't know where to start."

At the bewilderment in her voice, he took her hand in his. He couldn't stop himself from touching her. "Any-where you like."

She offered him a tentative smile, then took a deep breath. "I was breaking my fast with my grandfather this morning. He was playing with me as if he were a tomcat, and I a field mouse." She shook her head. "Though he didn't tell me outright, he's become aware that Alice is carrying. He plans to humiliate her, then throw her out onto the street."

"She's welcome to stay here until she and Benjamin marry. Two more banns need to be announced." His gaze met hers. "If your grandfather demands she repay her wages over the last month, I'll give her the coin."

"That won't help." She squeezed his hand as tears welled in her eyes. "My grandfather says my late grandmother's treasured silver teaspoon set is missing." She shook her head. "I do not doubt it will mysteriously appear in Alice's belongings." She thrust her reticule in his direction. "Open it, please."

He took the bag and pulled the drawstring open without taking his eyes from hers. He glanced at the contents and saw the glint of silver "These are the teaspoons?"

She nodded. "The queen gave them to my grandmother as a token of friendship. My grandmother valued them above all else because of their meaning."

"Then why do you have them?" He already suspected the answer, but he needed to ask her so she would tell him the rest of the story.

"Because it's a ruse my grandfather will use to have Alice transported. He'll say she stole them and use them as evidence." Celeste stared straight ahead, then turned to him with a sense of determination enveloping her. "I took them so that when the allegations are made, I can defend her."

She was not an ordinary woman of the *ton* who made social calls to be polite. Celeste Worsley made them to protect her loved ones.

She was fierce, and he'd never seen her more beautiful. Though frightened, she came here to shield her lady's maid. Most women of her ilk wouldn't even blink if their maid was transported. They'd take an inventory of their jewelry to ensure it was all safe, then hire another servant to replace the one they'd lost. The kind of loyalty and friendship Celeste exhibited toward Alice was extraordinarily special. It was truly amazing since the differences between the two women were stark not only in terms of class but also in terms of power. But Celeste didn't even seem to be bothered by any of that.

"Why are you choosing to be involved with this? I thought you were trying to please your grandfather so he and your parents would reconcile?"

Her gaze drifted to the window overlooking the courtyard. The nervous energy around her had seemed to double if the agitated twitch of her fingers was any indication. After a quiet moment, she shook her head as if shaking off her trepidation. "Alice was my only friend when my grandfather paid for my boarding school. I took her with me. Other young ladies attended with their maids as well. Naturally, they all knew about the estrangement between my parents and my grandfather." She rolled her eyes. "Lady Honoria and Lady Pippa weren't cruel. But the majority treated me as if I'd been estranged from him as well, even though he was the one who paid my tuition. When snide looks came my way, Alice comforted me."

He'd never seen her so defensive. He knew the feeling. They were alike in so many ways. She had a benefactor, and because of that, she was looked down upon. So was he. But his benefactor was kind and gracious. Her grandfather was the definition of cantankerous.

"To answer your other question about my involvement in this, I owe this to Alice. When I was far from home without a friend, having someone who looks out for me was essential to my well-being. And for me, that person was Alice. She always warned me to avoid situations that could lead to embarrassment or being ostracized." She studied her hands clasped in her lap, then turned her enticing green gaze his way.

He lowered his voice. "What kind of embarrassing situations?"

"Gossip and such." She sighed. "Most of the students believed that I thought myself better than them." She laughed, but there was little humor in her voice. "You're not the first one to think me arrogant or call me duchess." She wrinkled her nose as if smelling something foul. "Frankly, I think it ironic that my fellow students called me such with disdain. They would relish such a name. Isn't that the ultimate prize for a young woman on the marriage mart? They all want to marry a duke, so they'll possess the moniker of a duchess."

He could see the hurt flash in her eyes as she shared how she learned to defend herself against others. When she delivered a haughty gaze a person's way, she wasn't judging them. She was protecting herself. How could he not have seen that when they attended the same social affairs?

"I call you duchess as a term of admiration."

She slid her gaze in his direction with a slight smile. "Of course you do," she challenged.

"And affection," he added. "If you prefer that I don't call you that, I shall cease."

She waved a hand between them. "Call me what you like."

Then and there, he decided that he'd only refer to her as duchess when they were alone and, preferably, when he was kissing her. It made him more determined to win her hand and gain her grandfather's approval.

He still held her reticule. "You should take this."

Celeste took it and laid it in her lap, where the

teaspoons rattled again. "My grandfather will probably have the housekeeper hide these in Alice's possessions. If I have them in my room, my grandfather's housekeeper will say Alice hid them there."

Such a statement proved how astute she was.

Celeste bit her bottom lip again, then ran her tongue over the tender flesh. "What shall I do with them?"

It would take little for him to lean over and pull that tender skin between his teeth, soothe it with his tongue, then kiss her until neither of them knew their names or where they came from. He groaned at the thought. That's what this kind, loyal, and amazing woman did for him. If she treated her servant with such love and respect, he could hardly fathom how she would treat her husband.

The thought sent a jolt of jealousy through him. The idea that Celeste Worsley would marry a man her grandfather picked out for her rankled every bone in his body. If she married some fop who didn't appreciate her beauty inside and out, Malcolm would challenge the imbecile to a duel.

He was turning into a brute at just the thought. He ran his hands through his blond hair as he tried to tame his wild musings. There was no cause for alarm. He'd already set in motion the plan to win her regard and her grandfather's respect. Once he had both, he'd ask for her hand in marriage. With his wealth and the esteem of his membership in Pelham's Millionaires Club, what man would deny him his granddaughter's hand in marriage? More importantly, he'd woo Celeste until she had no doubts that he was the man she wanted to marry.

What was the matter with him? She came to him for help, and all he could do was daydream about ravishing her with kisses and proving to her grandfather that he was the only man worthy of her hand.

"Forgive me," he said gently. "I was woolgathering. I have a large cast iron safe in my bedroom. Give the spoons to me. I'll keep them safe. I'll pay for a common license. Ben and Alice can marry next week."

"No more waiting for the banns." For the first time that day, she wore a genuine smile. "Oh, thank you, Malcolm. Let me pay half."

It wasn't often that a beautiful woman regarded him as if he were her knight errant. Her blazing smile and the flash of affection in her eyes made him feel ten feet tall.

"You don't have to pay me," he murmured, then caught himself. "On second thought, I do want something."

Her brow furrowed. "What's that?"

Instantly, he wanted to smooth his fingers until the line that creased between her brows disappeared. "I want you to dance the first waltz with me at Ravenscroft's ball."

"It would be my pleasure," she said softly.

He leaned near and studied a thousand shades of green in her brilliant eyes and thought of kaleidoscopes. "How about I give you even more pleasure."

"Do you want to show me more pleasure here or at the ball? What kind of pleasure should I expect?" Her eyes playfully widened.

He chuckled. "The pleasure I'm talking about is showing you the kittens."

You are a man who knows how to pleasure a woman." She winked.

If she only knew.

And he planned to show her someday.

CHAPTER SIX

I was hard to believe that the week had passed so quickly, and now Celeste was standing beside Alice as she married. Celeste slid a side-eye glance at Malcolm. With his hands clasped in front of him, he stood ramrod straight beside Benjamin. Frankly, he could have been the groom. With his navy wool morning coat with split tails, a matching brocade waistcoat, and buckskin breeches, he was the epitome of an English gentleman. Even wearing boots, he looked elegant. With his broad shoulders and slim waist, he was gorgeous. Surely, heaven would not blame her for admiring such a figure even if she was in a church.

As the vicar droned on about sickness, health, and eternity, Celeste took a moment to allow the holiness of the event to seep through. Two people who were madly in love with one another were pledging their troth before God and anyone else within listening distance. They were declaring their commitment to one another for however many days on this earth they shared. That love and commitment extended to their unborn child.

Celeste imagined that it was different from how her own parents must have married. Escaping to Gretna Green and marrying in front of a smithy didn't seem romantic, but perhaps it was as reverent and beautiful as this ceremony. The next time she was with them, she would ask about their wedding.

"I now pronounce you man and wife."

The vicar's scratchy voice rang through the church. She'd never cared for the words "man and wife." Why couldn't it simply be, "I now pronounce you a couple dedicated to each other." It seemed to her that the words were more appropriate when the newly married couple viewed each other as equals and totally pledged to ensure one another's happiness and health.

Celeste smiled slightly as Benjamin wrapped Alice in his arms and pressed a chaste kiss to her lips. Alice said something to him, and he nodded.

By then, Malcolm stood by her side. "It's time to sign the register. The vicar wants the newlyweds to sign first, then you and I." Without hesitating, he wrapped her arm around his, and they were escorted to a small vestibule off to the side of the sanctuary. An ancient register laid open on the table next to a writing stand that held a pot of ink and a sharpened quill.

Malcolm motioned for Celeste to sign first after Alice and Benjamin. She bent over and quickly signed her name where the vicar pointed. Malcolm took the pen from her, then grinned as he blotted the quill after dipping it in the pot of ink. He signed, then returned the quill to its proper place.

As the vicar offered his congratulations to the new couple, Malcolm leaned close. "Celeste Susan Worsley." He captured her gaze with a wry smile. "A very proper English name."

She wanted to roll her eyes but decided that it wouldn't be appropriate at such a solemn moment. "I was named after my mother. It's a tradition in our family that the daughter takes her mother's name as her middle name."

With his head tilted and his eyes serious, he nodded as if she'd just made a profound point.

She smiled at his expression. "It's just a name."

"But I take names very seriously, especially when it's yours." He winked, then turned his attention to the newlyweds. "Shall we adjourn to my home? Cook has outdone herself in preparing a feast for your wedding breakfast." Malcolm smiled at the vicar. "Of course, we'd be delighted if you could join as well, Mr. Merknight."

"Thank you, but the rector is coming by to discuss a few things about the parish." He turned to the happy couple. "Congratulations on a beautiful and joyous union."

He turned and left them standing in the vestibule.

"Mr. Hollandale, I apologize, but I think it best if Alice and I return home. She's feeling a little poorly." Benjamin placed his arm around her waist.

"Alice, what's wrong?" Celeste asked. Then she noticed her friend's pale complexion and the sweat that dotted her brow. She pulled out a handkerchief and gave it to her. "Would you like for me to come with you?"

"No, thank you," Alice murmured. "Mornings are not a good time for me to be out and about. I need to rest."

Celeste went to her side and placed a kiss on her cheek. "I'm so happy for you. Will you send me a note when you feel up to a visit?"

Alice nodded.

Celeste shook Benjamin's hand. "Take care of her and yourself."

"I plan to, Miss Worsley." Benjamin grinned, then shook Malcolm's hand. "Thank you, sir, for everything."

"It's my pleasure," Malcolm answered.

They all walked out the front door of the church and said their respective goodbyes. As the couple descended the church steps and made their way into the waiting carriage, Celeste tipped her head back. It was a hazy sky, but the sun peeked through the clouds promising a gorgeous day in their future.

"It was a beautiful ceremony, don't you think?" she asked.

"It was." Malcolm smiled, the tenderness on his face betrayed how affected he was by the couple pledging their troth to one another. He rocked back on his heels and regarded her. "It seems a shame that Cook went to all that trouble for the breakfast, and there's no one else except me to enjoy it."

"You have servants who eat, don't you?" Celeste teased.

He laughed gently as the lines around his warm eyes crinkled. It was a harbinger that this man knew how to laugh and did it often. It was one of the things she admired about him. He was in possession of a good and kind nature. "They've already eaten."

Her hand flew to her chest. "Are you inviting me to eat with you in your home?"

He narrowed his eyes and tilted his head as if contemplating her question. "I believe I am." He nodded with a smile. "Indeed. I would be honored if you would share the wedding breakfast with me."

With such a charming invitation, Celeste couldn't resist. "I accept." She frowned. She couldn't just waltz up to his house in Amelia's carriage. "Perhaps it best if I don't. I shouldn't be seen entering an unmarried man's house."

"What if you're not seen?" A wicked smile tugged at his lips, and his eyes flashed with a challenge.

Oh, she was never one to walk away from a challenge, but this was not the appropriate behavior of a lady. *But it's him*. That pesky voice inside asked her how many times she would have the opportunity to be alone with him.

If she weren't on the church steps, she'd curse her annoyance. But it didn't diminish the thrill that heated her blood and made her heart pound. Yes, she wanted to be alone with him.

Again.

"What are you thinking?" she asked nonchalantly.

"Well, if I have my driver tell yours that I'll see you home, you and I can ride in my carriage." He looked up and down the streets. "Traffic is almost non-existent. I'll pull the curtains and have the coach come around to the back of my house."

If it were her logical self, she'd say absolutely not. But it was her heart that said—no yelled—for her to take this chance and not look back. She'd always been the dutiful daughter and devoted granddaughter, and her time for enjoying her life was fast coming to an end. She could feel it. Without hesitating, she decided she would eat with him. An hour in his company wouldn't hurt anyone.

Especially if no one found out.

Malcolm couldn't tear his gaze from Celeste the entire time they were in the carriage. She wore a coral-colored morning gown trimmed in cream ribbon and seed pearls. With her black hair, green eyes, and perfect skin, she could have been a model for a Thomas Lawrence painting.

As the carriage came to a stop at the back entrance of his Palladian home, he sat on the edge of his seat. As his legs framed hers, he was struck by the intimacy of the moment. He was no virgin, but he'd never been this close to a woman in an enclosed space in his entire life. Her scent and the sound of her gown shifting were amplified in the coach. It would take nothing to lean her way and press a kiss upon her cheek.

Frankly, he didn't know if he could stop at just a simple kiss next time. "Ready? I hope you're hungry."

A knowing smile creased her lips. By the way she looked at him, she was well aware that he wasn't simply talking about food.

"I am hungry." Her voice had dropped into a deep alto that had the effect of a tuning fork on his body. Everything seemed to vibrate at once. He clenched one of his gloved hands, desperate to gain control over the unannounced departure of his poise. He took a deep breath and released it.

Her brow furrowed. "Is everything all right?"

All he wanted to do was to lay her down in the carriage and do unspeakable things to her. So, the answer to her question was no. Everything was not all right.

But somehow, he found the fortitude to smile. "Let's get you inside."

A footman opened the carriage door, and Malcolm exited. He turned and offered his hand to assist her. When she took it with such a gentle touch, he wanted to hiss at the undeniable spark that blazed between them.

As soon as she was on the ground, her rose fragrance wrapped itself around him, holding him hostage. His nostrils flared. Perhaps it hadn't been such a good idea to ask her to his home.

Celeste smiled up at him and then turned toward the

entrance. Her eyes widened as she saw his butler and housekeeper waiting for them. Both were practically bouncing on their toes. By the expressions on their faces, their excitement over his entertaining guests this morning practically made them giddy.

"They're expecting company. I hated to disappoint them." He winked.

What bollocks. Though he might be experiencing a bit of trepidation over his physical response to her, *he* wanted her here.

He lifted his hand in greeting. His butler, Simon, was in his mid-fifties. His white hair was in contrast to his elegant black morning coat with matching breeches and waistcoat. His housekeeper, Mrs. Morris, was a tad younger. She wore a simple black muslin gown with a cream-colored fichu and a matching cap. She wore a sterling chatelaine with keys around her waist. The woman sounded like miniature church bells when she walked.

He and Celeste stopped in front of the two servants. Simon bowed and Mrs. Morris curtseyed.

"Miss Worsley, this is Edgar Simon, my butler, and Mrs. Morris, my housekeeper."

"How do you do?" Celeste asked politely.

"Very well, ma'am," the butler offered. "It's lovely to have you at Takeley House."

"Indeed." Mrs. Morris beamed, then turned to Malcolm. "Sir, where are the other guests?"

"I'm afraid the bride wasn't feeling well."

"The poor dear," Mrs. Morris clucked in sympathy. "I'm sure Benjamin will take good care of her."

That tidbit instantly brought a smile to Celeste's face. "You have a good opinion of Mr. Brannan?"

"Indeed, Miss Worsley." Mrs. Morris clasped her

hands in front of her. "And I've heard wonderful things about his Alice as well. I'm anxious to meet her."

Celeste was beaming. He stood there staring at her as the sight robbed him of breath. She was stunning in her joy.

Completely oblivious to the effect she was having on him, Celeste continued to smile at his butler and housekeeper. "You'll be enchanted by her. You will never meet anyone more honest or truer than Alice."

Both servants nodded with matching smiles.

"The dining room is prepared for you and your guest, sir," Simon said, then walked up the five steps and opened the door to Malcolm's home.

He took Celeste's arm and escorted her inside the anteroom. As soon as she entered, her mouth fell open. "I expected we'd enter the kitchen. I never dreamed you would have a beautiful room here." She tilted her head to the ceiling and gazed at the doomed ceiling decorated with Greek gods and goddesses guarding the entrance. Malcolm thought the blue porcelain and white room a little gaudy, but if Celeste liked it, perhaps he needed to study it a bit more carefully.

"Well, Miss Worsley, I don't know if Mr. Hollandale told you, but this manse used to belong to the Duke of Takeley. It was built in 1710. The duke had Mr. Robert Adam redesign the interior in 1761. Magnificent, isn't it, Miss?" Simon rocked on his heels with a smug smile of satisfaction.

"Oh my, yes," Celeste said softly as she turned in a circle before her gaze found his. "Your home makes me speechless."

"Well, we can't have that, Miss Worsley," Malcolm teased with a grin. "Otherwise, it will be a very boring wedding breakfast for me."

She smiled, and a beautiful blush colored her cheeks. She fit in perfectly here. He was overjoyed that she appreciated his house.

He just hoped she liked him as much as the anteroom.

As Simon and Mrs. Morris took their leave, Malcolm threaded their fingers together as he led the way to the dining room. "Come, duchess."

She slowed her step and regarded him.

By the flash of heat in her direct gaze, she was definitely engaged.

And it definitely wasn't just her interest in eating.

She was most certainly interested in him.

Celeste followed Malcolm from the anteroom through a small passageway with two open doors. A music room designed in an Etruscan style was on her right. A pianoforte stood in front of the floor-to-ceiling windows with a sitting area surrounding it.

There was no doubt that she was gawking, but how could she not? His home was divine. It should be a museum, not where a mortal man lived.

"This is my study. Have a look if you'd like." His voice was calm and not at all boastful. If she thought his workplace was splendid, his Mayfair home could only be considered grandly resplendent.

She stole a peek inside, and the study was more impressive than any other room she'd seen thus far. Light poured through the windows showcasing the massive bookcases that lined the entire room. The entire room was painted in creams, beiges, and pale yellows. Spiral staircases led to an open second floor that was lined with books.

"Oh, Malcolm," she whispered in awe.

"You don't think it too ostentatious?" He smirked as he looked around the room, then at her.

"I think it's perfect." She nodded her approval.

"I'm glad you like it. It's my favorite room." He waved a hand to the next room. "This is my second favorite." He opened the door and motioned for her to precede him.

As soon as she stepped through, she stopped. The formal dining room seemed to glow. The walls were covered in cream-colored silk. Windows ran the entire length of two walls. They were framed on either side by gilded pier mirrors and matching console tables. The cost of the window tax for this one room would bankrupt most peers. But the pièce de resistance was the massive table that stood in the middle of the room. Food was everywhere. Dishes of oysters, scrambled eggs with flakes of truffles, cream cakes, stuffed cucumbers, cooked artichokes, strawberries, fresh tarts, biscuits, creamy butter, and honey, along with fresh ham and crispy bacon, kippers, and an assortment of fresh fruit sat upon the table in a porcelain pink and gold china set. There was so much food that it was difficult to see what color the table covering was.

Two footmen pulled out chairs at the end of the table for them.

"Thank you, John and Ian. We can serve ourselves." Malcolm stood at the head of the table and held out the chair to his immediate right for her.

"Very well, Mr. Hollandale." The two footmen filed out of the room, quietly closing the door behind them.

Malcolm waited until she sat before he scooted her chair toward the table. But he didn't sit down. Instead, he picked up several dishes and placed them in front of their seats. "My favorites," he said as he lifted his eyebrows with a grin. "I hope they're yours as well."

"You have enough to feed Wellington's army." She laughed. "I don't even know what half of these dishes are."

"I wasn't certain what you liked." He placed a stuffed cucumber and several oysters on her plate, then served himself. His movements were graceful and completely at ease. Meanwhile, she was as fidgety as the kitten One at play.

Her cheeks heated. They had to match the dark pink of the plates. "I'm sure you meant you didn't know what Alice and Benjamin would like."

With a slight movement that could only be called economical, he put the serving spoon down, then leaned near. He slowly blinked as he regarded her. His ridiculously long lashes brushed his skin in a caress.

"No. I meant you." His low voice thrummed through her entire body.

"Oh." What an absolutely inane response to make. She sounded like a schoolgirl with her first infatuation. Her movements slowed as she considered the man sitting next to her. She certainly wasn't a schoolgirl anymore, but he was definitely someone who had her notice and had for quite a long time.

Why were men such as he, who already had a bounty of beauty, given such handsome attributes? But really, his lashes were perfect. They matched his full lips. With his blond hair, sun-kissed skin, and perfect form, he reminded her of a relaxing lion who twitched its tail as it contemplated whether it was worth his time to go after the prey in front of him. She should be afraid. Instead, a thrill shot through her that he relished her company.

"Are you flirting with me?" she murmured.

"Perhaps," he purred like a predator on the prowl. "Shall we eat?"

She straightened in her chair at the intimacy they shared. She'd never been this...alone...with anyone before. Every one of her senses was alert, anticipating what might happen next.

"I've never eaten alone with a man before," she blurted out softly. "This is a first for me."

He poured red wine into her glass as he regarded her and poured the appropriate amount.

How did he do that without spilling a drop? His gaze never left hers as if she was the most important thing in his world at that moment. Malcolm Hollandale was utterly charming, more so than any other person she'd ever met in her life.

"Don't you eat with your grandfather?" he asked.

"There are always footmen."

He nodded. "I don't want you uncomfortable. If things had worked out differently, Alice and Benjamin would have joined us. Would you like for me to ask a footman to remain in the room with us?" Their gazes met. "Say the word, and I'll call them both back."

"No." It was incredibly sweet the way he looked out for her. "I was just making an observation."

"I also have an observation." His voice was low and purposely mysterious. "I've never eaten alone with a woman either."

She was in the process of taking a sip of wine and practically choked on it. She widened her eyes and regarded him.

"Except..." He smiled like a libertine who was proud of it.

For some unknown reason, the thought that someone else had shared such an intimacy with Malcolm rankled her moment of happiness. She slowly set down her wine glass and regarded him.

Then he winked at her. "Except for my mother."

A small laugh bubbled inside her.

"And Mrs. Cat."

She had no idea whether it was because they were in the room alone and making light of it or perhaps it was because he simply put her at ease. Her laughter grew until he joined in. After a few moments, she couldn't control it any longer. She laughed so hard and for so long that her stomach muscles protested. Without thinking, she placed her hand over his. "Stop, I beg of you."

He took her hand in his, then shook his head. "Need I remind you that you started it with your *observation*."

"Guilty as charged, sir."

She began to pull her hand away, but his grip tightened, and he brought it to his mouth. "You're a joy to be around."

That telltale heat rose on her cheeks again. Would she ever quit being bashful when he said sweet things to her?

Gently, he let go of her hand. He picked up his wine glass and studied it by deftly twirling the stem between his fingers. "You deserve compliments, duchess."

"Thank you," she murmured.

After taking a sip of wine, he set the glass down. He held an oyster shell, then brought it to his mouth. The long muscles of his neck lengthened and undulated as he swallowed. The man even made eating a common mollusk look sensually elegant.

She picked up the stuffed cucumber and brought it to her mouth. It was small in size and filled with cream and dill. She took a bite, then moaned at the juxtaposition of the different textures and flavors. "This is divine. I love the hardness and the creaminess. It just explodes on your tongue."

When she sucked the end and put it in her mouth for another bite, Malcolm's nostrils flared, and his gaze narrowed. "You do that rather well."

"What?" she asked innocently.

"Sucking hard things," he murmured.

She tilted her head and regarded him. After a moment, it dawned on her what he might be referring to. Alice had told her about pleasuring Benjamin by putting his... in her mouth and sucking. Her gaze dipped to the table, where she gently put the remaining cucumber on her plate. She didn't know whether to be offended, mortified, or snicker with laughter. It was all rather naughty.

His gaze was glued to his plate, but it didn't hide the mischievous grin that pulled on his full lips. The urge to lean across the table and bite his plump bottom lip came from nowhere.

"This meal seems to have the potential for turning into a ribald wedding breakfast," she murmured.

His gaze flew to hers. "I assume you mean something humorous."

"You, sir, are incorrigible." She shook her head in playful admonishment.

He lifted both hands as if surrendering. "I meant no offense, duchess. May I ask you a question?" He waited for her nod before continuing. "When you said the word potential, I thought of the future. How do you see yours unfolding?"

She took a deep breath and released it before leaning back in her chair and regarding him. "Marriage."

"That's your goal?" He played with his wine glass. His large hand enveloped the fragile cut glass with ease. She had no doubt that he could crush it with his bare hands, but he was being incredibly careful with it. Just like he would be with any person he cared for.

What if he cared for her?

No, she couldn't have such thoughts. Malcolm Hollandale was not for her. At least, he was an acquaintance. At most, he was a friend.

"Marriage isn't a goal. It's a task. A means to an end." She leaned forward and took a sip of wine.

Locking his gaze with hers, he elegantly ate another oyster. Afterward, he placed an oyster shell on her plate. He speared the oyster with his fork and brought it to her lips. "Taste." She was about to side-eye him when he continued, "It's delicious with a bit of horseradish and pepper sauce."

She opened her mouth and closed her eyes. The cold, slippery texture almost made her grimace until the spices exploded in her mouth. She swallowed and widened her eyes. "That's good."

He nodded with a quick smile. "Delicious?"

"If one is a connoisseur of mollusks."

He laughed and put another oyster on her plate, then refilled her glass.

She hadn't noticed, but he was serving her, feeding her, like a male raptor taking care of his mate. It was incredibly tender and sweet on his part.

He rested his chin in his palm as he regarded her. "Do tell me what you mean by marriage as a means to an end."

She shrugged slightly. "It's simple. Once a woman marries and produces the requisite heir or two, she's met the requirements for most husbands of the *ton*. Once that obligation is met, she can live her own life."

"I see." He dipped a spoon into a small bowl of honey. Without dripping any, he brought it to her mouth. "Taste," he commanded.

"I don't do well with commands," she retorted softly.

"I'm flirting," he answered.

With her heart beating fast, she stared into his eyes. His pupils had dilated, and somehow, their chairs had moved closer together.

Never taking her gaze from his, she took the spoon from his hand, then put it in her mouth and sucked. The sweet taste of clover and summer melded together on her tongue. She closed her eyes and sighed in pleasure.

"Duchess, you have a rather jaded view of matrimony, particularly after the beautiful ceremony we saw today between two people in love. Don't you want more from your marriage?" The timbre of his voice was as smooth and sweet as the honey he'd given her.

"Such as?" She licked the spoon, not wanting to waste a drop.

"Companionship?"

"I could get a dog or a cat."

He laughed. "Could you get"—he played with his wine glass again, then gaze directly at her before it fell to her lips—"touches that warmed you from the inside out and made you yearn for more?" Again, he lowered his voice until it reminded her of liquid gold—warm, smooth, and rich. "Caresses that make you hunger for more?"

Her entire body felt heated. She squeezed her thighs together, hoping for relief from the ache that resided there.

He reached over and swept his finger across her lower lip. "You left a little honey."

She opened her mouth in invitation. A wicked smile appeared on his lips as his finger touched her tongue. Instantly, she closed her mouth and sucked deep. She wrapped her tongue around his finger and stared into his eyes. When they widened, she clasped his wrist with her hand and held him close, all the while sucking and stroking his finger, relishing the taste of honey and Malcolm Hollandale on her tongue.

"Don't you want your husband's eyes to stare at you so intensely that you feel the heat of his gaze within every part of you?" His gaze boldly raked over her. "I think you'll be the type of wife who will reveal all her softness only with someone she trusts."

Celeste continued to suck his finger as her arousal grew, listening to the slow languid seduction of his voice. She had no doubt that the man before her knew how to ease her ache.

She let go of his finger and licked her own lips. "You make me want those things," she said softly.

"You once told me that you gave up all those dreams. But you did everything you could for Alice." He leaned close and rubbed his nose against hers. "Such a sweet sentiment, duchess."

His sandalwood scent drugged her senses. She opened her mouth slightly, readying herself for his kiss.

Like the touch of a butterfly's wings, he pressed his lips to hers. "Give in to all your desires, duchess. I'm certain there's a man out there who wants to give it all to you and more."

They were innocent words, but the nuances were bursting with promises that made her ache even more. She nodded, almost whispering the word yes. Her eyes fluttered open at the same time that reason barged into her thoughts, scattering his seduction like autumn leaves caught by the north wind.

She leaned back. Malcolm's gaze was locked with hers. She did want everything, but to even consider it would lead to heartache for her parents, not to mention herself. She'd feel like a failure if she couldn't help them.

She couldn't be selfish and only think of herself and her own wants and needs.

Yet, this was a moment in time that she knew she'd cherish forever. Not only was she celebrating Alice and Benjamin's union, but she was living her favorite fantasy. Malcolm Hollandale was seducing her. She could pretend he was hers and she was his.

It was enough.

It had to be enough.

"I should be going. It's getting late." She pushed away and glanced at the length of the table. "Such an eclectic serving of foods." She turned to look into his eyes. "How did you come up with it?"

His gaze locked on hers so fiercely she might believe that he had thrown away the key. "I prepared the menu."

She couldn't answer. Nor could she look away. The heat, the warmth, and the comfort he suggested earlier was in his gaze.

"Celeste, before I tell you how I picked the menu, there's one other thing I forgot to mention. Care." His voice dropped to a growl. "Care. Your future husband should care for you." He cupped her cheek. "He should protect you when the world is harsh."

She swallowed as her emotions threatened to riot. "You've given me quite a lot to consider."

"Good." His blue eyes bored into hers, promising her everything she had ever wanted. "The food I fed you? I chose them as they are considered aphrodisiacs."

She released a tremulous breath.

Now she knew.

Pretending that she was his and he was hers would never be enough.

CHAPTER SEVEN

"Hollandale, it's an honor to have you here," Hugh Calthorpe, the Marquess of Ravenscroft, shook Malcolm's hand.

A bit taller than Malcolm's six-foot two-inch frame, the marquess could only be described as good-humored but sharp as an ax. He could cut someone into pieces with a laugh and a comment without the other person knowing they'd been skewered. Such was the wit of the Marquess of Ravenscroft, the host of tonight's ball.

He was the opposite of Malcolm. Whereas Malcolm had blond hair and a lithe but athletic build, the marquess had black hair and a muscular build. It was a testament to the hard physical labor he enjoyed on his ancestral seat and at his estate near the Jolly Rooster. He and Trafford owned estates close to the Duke of Pelham's ducal seat.

"Pelham and Trafford are here. They'll be as delighted as I am to see you. It's been too long, my friend."

"What are you on about, Ravenscroft?" Malcolm laughed. "I just saw you several days ago at Ardeerton House."

Ravenscroft leaned near so that his mother, the hostess of the ball, couldn't overhear the conversation. "If you had to live here while your mother planned a ball on your behalf, you'd lose track of time as well. Purgatory is just another word for soiree planning."

"It sounds like a delightful way to spend time with your mother. You're lucky she's living with you." Malcolm meant every word. Family was a gift, and he looked forward to starting one. The sooner, the better, in his opinion.

"She keeps me on my toes." Ravenscroft winked, then leaned a bit closer and lowered his voice. "Just a fair warning. Pelham's two sisters are here."

"Lady Honoria is her? I've never met her."

"No one has. First time out in society. I think it's safe to say he has a watchful eye over them. Every time a man comes near, I swear I can hear the man growling from across the room." The marquess's eyes twinkled with mirth. "Therefore, I plan on asking both to dance with me just to upset the man. You should do the same."

"You're a braver person than me," Malcolm said with a grin. "However, it's always entertaining when the duke experiences something not quite to his liking."

"Indeed." Ravenscroft nodded. "Lady Grace Webster is in attendance as well."

Malcolm stole a glance at the attendees.

It was common knowledge that Pelham and Lady Grace could not be in the same room at the same time without barbs, sharper than rapiers, being thrown in both directions. No one in the *ton* understood why. Lady Grace and Pelham never discussed it.

"Has something happened that I don't know about?" Malcolm asked.

Ravenscroft shrugged. "I believe that she's helping

Lady Honoria and Trafford. You didn't hear it from me, but I think there may be an understanding between them."

"Interesting," Malcolm said, then smiled.

Ravenscroft nodded. "Lady Grace could help you with Miss Worsley. She's been known to matchmake for a select few."

"I'll keep that in mind," Perhaps Lady Grace could help him win the Duke of Exehill's regard. With a nod, he took his leave of the marquess and meandered among the other guests who'd already arrived.

As Malcolm stepped into the ballroom, the air changed, and he inhaled deeply. She was here. He hadn't located Celeste Worsley, but everything around him seemed to shimmer in anticipation. Ever since the wedding breakfast, all he could think about was her. Though Malcolm didn't possess a title. He possessed something much more valuable.

Money.

Many aristocrats were property-rich but cash poor. Fortunately for Malcolm, he was rich in both. However, that still didn't negate the rebuffs and outright snubs he received from the *ton* members who disapproved of people who made money the old-fashioned way as Malcolm did. He earned everything he had by spending long hours experimenting and designing new ways to improve people's lives.

If the *ton* had its way, Malcolm should turn tail and run. But that was not him. He'd worked at experiments until he found success and exceeded everyone's expectations. He never quit. He had a clever mind, a handsome build, and a pleasant enough face that people did a double take. Besides that, he was rich and an original member of Pelham's Millionaires Club. None of that appeared to matter. He was still regarded as a Cit, a commoner, a man of trade. As he looked around the ballroom at the various members of the aristocracy, one thing became readily apparent. He had more money than most of the men here. But they only saw him as common, and not as anything close to an equal.

Damn them all to hell.

Yet, he was once again attending another boring *ton* function. Insults would be delicately thrown in his direction. Tonight, he'd tolerate it and keep his anger under control.

The only reason? Because *his duchess* was here.

When he captured his first glimpse of her, he stood taller and, without hesitating, made his way across the ballroom. He'd not embarrass her by giving her any special attention. He'd treat her just as he would any other society miss. He'd be attentive, curious but not effusive in his conversation.

If he wanted Celeste Worsley as his, he needed to play the long game, as Pelham had told him time and time again. The wedding breakfast had proven it. He'd seen the doubt in her eyes about marriage as a task when he'd talked to her. She was the type of woman who would love a man completely. He hungered like a starving man for her to accept him on his terms, which meant coming to him.

And once she did? Then, he wouldn't wait to hold her in his arms and sweep her across the dance floor. Perhaps tonight he could convince her to walk with him through Ravenscroft's gardens. He had to tell her the latest antics of the kittens.

And perchance steal another kiss or two.

Celeste only half listened to her friends Lady Anne Vickery and Lady Beatrice Sutton as they all chatted about Lady Honoria Ardeerton, the oldest sister of the Duke of Pelham. A buzz of excitement filled the air, which could only be attributed to the fact that the elusive Lady Honoria had finally come to London, and a rumor hummed through the *ton* that she and Lord Trafford were going to announce their engagement this very evening.

Frankly, it didn't interest Celeste in the slightest. There was only one thing...or she should say one person...who caught her attention. Currently, he was striding in her direction.

She took a deep breath and smiled. It had been mere days since she'd last seen Malcolm, but it felt like weeks. Heat bloomed in her cheeks as he came toward her. Everything he'd said to her at the wedding breakfast was committed to memory. How could it not? That's what she wanted in a husband, but she considered herself a realist. She would not have that in her marriage.

Once he made his way to their group, Malcolm greeted everyone, then turned to her with a smile. "Miss Worsley."

"Mr. Hollandale." She felt as jumpy as one of his playful kittens. How could a simple smile make her dizzy? Thankfully, she remembered not to call him Malcolm in front of the group.

The Earl of Carlyle, another member of the Duke of Pelham's Millionaire Club, had joined their group along with the elusive Lady Honoria. Celeste didn't stand idle. She was friends with Lady Honoria and would make her presence known.

"Gracious, Lady Honoria, it's so wonderful to see you in London."

Honoria squeezed her arm affectionately. "Celeste, seeing a familiar friend in the crowd is always welcome."

Lord Carlyle frowned in her direction. In answer, Malcolm glared at the earl, then sidled next to Celeste and Honoria. "Miss Worsley, will you introduce me to your friend?"

Before she could open her mouth, Carlyle did the honors with his nose tilted toward the ceiling as if Malcolm wasn't good enough to share his rarefied air. "Lady Honoria, may I present Mr. Malcolm Hollandale."

"My lady," Malcolm said as he executed a formal bow.

Celeste's breath caught at his graceful move. But she shouldn't be surprised. Everything he did was elegant.

As he and Honoria chatted, Celeste evaluated Malcolm's stance. He wasn't standing as close to Honoria as he was to her. It was almost as if he were making a claim or trying to shield her from Carlyle. He need not bother. Lord Carlyle was someone she tried to ignore. To say he was unpleasant was an understatement.

"May I have the next dance?" Malcolm asked.

Celeste's heartbeat tripped in her chest. He was claiming his waltz with her. She turned quickly to face him, only to be staring at his back.

"Now, see here, Hollandale. Lady Honoria's next dance is mine," Carlyle protested. The fury in the man's voice could be heard throughout the ballroom.

His angry outburst grew faint as Celeste realized what had happened. Her cheeks heated from assuming that Malcolm was asking her to dance with him. After all, he'd asked for her first dance. Perhaps he'd forgotten. She frowned slightly. Perhaps it meant he wasn't as taken with her as she was with him. Hoping that no one caught her misstep, she closed her eyes. Good God, she was completely mortified.

How could she be so naïve as to think she'd be the only woman Malcolm would dance with this evening? It was expected that he'd ask Lady Honoria Ardeerton, the eldest sister of the Duke of Pelham, to accompany him. He was friends with Lady Honoria's brother, besides the fact that she was an heiress and a true beauty. Since she preferred the country over the city, it was little wonder she was popular this evening. Tonight marked the night of her first appearance in a London ballroom.

As Celeste smoothed her hand down her gown and feigned a smile, Lord Trafford headed their way with his hands clenched into fists. His expression guaranteed he was a man on a mission, and Celeste wagered that the mission had to do with rescuing Lady Honoria from Lord Carlyle's embarrassing behavior.

As soon as Lord Trafford arrived by Lady Honoria's side, he asked, "May I?" Without hesitating, he took her dance card and wrote his name in every available spot.

"What are you about, Trafford," Carlyle retorted.

"I'm claiming every one of Lady Honoria's dances as my own." Lord Trafford smiled at Honoria, then bowed toward Celeste. "Miss Worsley, if you'll excuse Lady Honoria and I?"

Malcolm's lips spread into a wide grin before he laughed. "Trafford, that's what I admire about you. You've always gotten what you want."

Trafford shook Malcolm's hand and laughed.

It didn't escape Celeste's notice that all the members of Pelham's Millionaires Club in attendance welcomed Malcolm with a true sense of affection and friendship.

That is, except for Lord Carlyle, who was the definition of sour grapes. The Earl of Carlyle huffed his displeasure loud enough that half of the ballroom could hear him.

When Lord Trafford swept Lady Honoria onto the dance floor, Malcolm leaned near. "May I have this dance?"

"You're very kind, but I don't mind introducing you to more of my friends." The merriment in his eyes caught her off-balance. "You could dance with one of them."

"That's not what I want, Celeste," He practically purred. "I saw Trafford heading toward our group as soon as I met Lady Honoria. I had to ask Lady Honoria to dance just to ruffle Lord Carlyle's feathers. You see, Lord Trafford has set his sights on Lady Honoria." His eyes blazed with a singular focus on her as he leaned nearer. "Truthfully, I wanted you. But I don't want to force my company on you," he said with a smile.

"Why would you think that?" Celeste forced herself to breathe evenly and regarded him. "If we're speaking truthfully, every time I've come to these events, I've wanted your company and attention." Good heavens, she was spilling all her thoughts and dreams to him again. But she couldn't help herself. For the first time ever, she thought of no one else except herself and him. It was humiliating to say such things, but what if she never got another chance? He was flirting with her, and she needed him to understand that it wasn't a game to her. "I hope that doesn't make you ill at ease in my company. I meant what I said. I will introduce you to others."

His eyes darkened as he stood close. She could feel the heat radiating from his body. "I regret that I didn't know your feelings, duchess. Let's forget about wife candidates for the evening. He took her hand and brought it to his lip. "Grant me a boon; make me the happiest man here tonight. Dance with me?"

When Malcolm Hollandale smiled as if his entire world revolved around her, she couldn't refuse such a request. She nodded her assent and allowed him to take her to the center of the dance floor.

"Is your grandfather here?" Malcolm murmured as the

first notes of a waltz trilled about them. He quickly swept her into his arms, then moved so effortlessly they could have been dancing on a cloud. "I'd like to be introduced to him."

"He was playing whist with several of his cronies in the card room." Celeste's hand rested on his shoulder. "I am certain he's left by now. He always leaves after an hour. I have a chaperone standing over there with the other matrons. She never even looks to see what I'm doing." She couldn't resist flexing her fingers on his hard muscles and was rewarded when his shoulder slightly undulated beneath her hands.

"Do you like touching me?" His steady gaze met hers in a silent demand she answer truthfully.

She dipped her head to escape his stare. She'd just squeezed him like a hothouse orange. What was the matter with her?

"Celeste?"

No one had ever called her missish when she had made a faux pas. Even though she was embarrassed, she forced her gaze to meet his.

He bit his lower lip, then squeezed her hand. "You didn't answer my question. Allow me to say that I feel the same about you. I don't think I can keep my hands off you either."

For a moment, she stared. When this handsome, unsettling man touched her, possibilities that she shouldn't consider, much less want, brewed like a witch's potion. His eyes danced with pleasure, and a grin tugged the corners of his mouth. Simply put, she was caught in his web of seduction. She could no more leave his side than she could walk to the moon. She shook her head to hide her mirth, but it failed. "You are too bold, sir."

"You like me that way." He expertly turned her to avoid another couple who careened toward them.

Unfortunately for Celeste, she did want to explore Malcolm's world. If her destiny was to marry some unknown man personally picked by her grandfather, couldn't she at least experience a flirtation or even a brief love affair with the man who held her heart in his hand?

If Malcolm Hollandale was her husband....

Celeste couldn't deny it any longer. With him, she was more honest, more alive, more eager to experience new things. She wasn't playing a part. She was allowing herself to be real for the first time since she'd arrived in London. Malcolm's most remarkable traits were his kindness, humor, and sense of honor. He used that honor to protect Benjamin, Alice, and their unborn baby. She wanted to explore everything she desired with Malcolm. It wasn't because of the magic of the night. It was more. For heaven's sake, the man lived with cats.

The man loved cats.

He was perfect.

But she could not think of the possibility of marriage to such a man. Her grandfather would only pick Malcolm if he were a duke and would do her grandfather's bidding.

In the time she'd spent with Malcolm, it was apparent he didn't do anyone's bidding unless he wanted to.

As the music slowed, she and Malcolm came to a stop, but he didn't let go of her hand. Instead, he wrapped it around his arm. "Come with me."

Without hesitating, Celeste turned and walked out a set of French doors that framed one ballroom wall. Once outside, she took a deep breath of the sweet scents surrounding her. There had to be thousands of blooming flowers in the courtyard below them.

As Malcolm led her down the terrace steps, several

other couples were enjoying the night's fresh air. Malcolm nodded at one couple, but he didn't stop to chat. Instead, he continued down the path toward a small bubbling fountain in the courtyard.

"Where are we going?" she said softly.

"To a secret spot that only I know how to enter." He tilted his head sideways toward her, then lowered his voice. "Are you game for a little adventure?"

"With you?" Before he could answer, she squeezed his forearm and continued, "Always, if I'm with you."

"That's my duchess," he whispered affectionally.

They continued walking until they entered a part of the courtyard where a blooming riot of climbing roses sprawled over several trellises. Wisteria and weeping willow trees surrounded them in a half circle. A stone wall with a door stood directly in front of them. It was private but open at the same time, with a delightful scent that reminded Celeste of her favorite perfumery in London.

"This is beautiful," she murmured as she twirled slowly to see the entire landscape.

"It's one of my favorite places in London. Ravenscroft has an excellent gardening staff, and his mother also enjoys gardening. Come. I want to show you this." Malcolm pushed the door open, then took her hand.

As soon as they were through the entrance, he stopped her so she could face him. It was as if they were in their own garden, surrounded by three stone walls completely covered in glorious green ivy. Where the fourth wall should have been, it was open and facing a side of the house where a beautiful terrace sitting area reigned over them.

"There's something I want to discuss with you...." She let the words trail off as the beauty of their surroundings came into focus.

"What's that?" Malcolm pulled her closer until their chests met.

Like the little white kitten she'd fallen in love with, Celeste rubbed her chest against his as if begging to be petted.

"I'll still introduce you to my friends and encourage their interests." She lifted her gaze, desperate for him to understand how much this meant to her. "But I want something more in our bargain."

He shook his head. "We agreed not to discuss this. Why would I when I have the most beautiful woman in the ballroom in my arms. A woman I want to kiss."

She couldn't look away from the intensity in his eyes. He practically smoldered when he looked at her. A blaze of desire burned between them and she wanted to get closer to the flame.

Malcolm slowly cupped her cheeks, his thumbs softly caressing her skin. "You do know that this is a terrible way to negotiate. We've already come to an agreement between us."

He pressed his lips against hers. She leaned against him and ran her fingers through his hair in response. When she tried to deepen the kiss, he pulled away, earning a heartfelt groan of disapproval from her.

"Tell me what it is," he murmured.

Slightly dizzy and flummoxed from his mesmerizing lips, Celeste blinked. "Teach me everything you know about desire."

By the look on Malcolm's face, now he was the one befuddled. He slowly pulled away and studied her. "What do you mean?"

Celeste pulled him closer. "Kissing, touching, and all that entails desire between people who are attracted to one another."

"And what about the man your grandfather will have you marry?" Malcolm played with a loose lock of her hair. His eyes boldly raked over her.

Perhaps she wasn't thinking through the implications thoroughly. But who could when his eyes burned with the promise of pleasure that only he could provide her? She chewed on her lip. Her grandfather would disown her if he knew what she was thinking. But this was a chance to experience the sweetness of Malcolm's kisses, the warmth of his embrace, and the care he'd give her tonight. Ever since their wedding breakfast together, he and all his promises were at the forefront of all her thoughts.

She should be scared to take what she wanted. Her poor parents had suffered because of their rash decisions. Yet, they loved each other then and were still madly in love. If there was true affection between her and Malcolm, then how could it be wrong to share each other's passion?

The only answer was that it wasn't. Then and there, she decided not to allow her grandfather's strict edicts to intrude tonight. Not when she had Malcolm's complete attention under this glorious moonlight.

The warmth of his heavy body against hers grounded her. It gave her the courage to meet his gaze and to tell her deepest wishes. "It's my body. I should have the right to choose. If I have to give up my dream of marrying for love, I want to experience it with someone I trust and admire. I want to experience it with you. I want you. I've always wanted you. Whatever I am and whatever I have now, I want to share it with you. I hope you'll do the same with me."

CHAPTER EIGHT

C eleste could have knocked Malcolm over with a feather duster at that moment. If she was asking what he thought she was, the lady standing before him wanted him to ruin her. He could not have heard her correctly.

"I don't know if that's wise," he whispered. Lanterns surrounded the gardens, lending a golden hue that washed over her face making her more enticing than Venus. The soft glow provided enough light to see that she was blushing.

"If it is too much to ask, I understand. I've never asked for anything like this. But you see... Alice shared with me how she feels when she's with Benjamin." She rested her hand against his heart and stared at it intently. "I want that, and tonight with you might be my only chance."

Without second-guessing himself, he placed his hand over hers. "What they have is beautiful."

She nodded her agreement. "I'll never have that. But I want to experience sharing my physical body with someone I care for." Slowly, she lifted her gaze to his. "I trust you."

Everything about her enchanted him. Her eyes made a man want to drown in them. Her slight curves begged to be touch right here in the garden. And her gown? It should be outlawed for indecency. It hugged her breasts as if wanting to torture him. But her scent was what drove him wild. Sweet roses demanding to be enjoyed. Their pink petals filled with warmth and dew as they wait for someone to separate their folds.

God, he was making himself hard just thinking about her.

It almost choked him to say the words, but he couldn't live with himself unless he tried to stop this. "What about the man you marry? You could fall in love with him."

She shrugged slightly, but her gaze never left his. "I could, but I don't know who it will be. For all I know, my grandfather may pick one of his cronies for me to marry." She shivered slightly.

"God, I'm sorry." Instinctively, he pulled her in closer to him and pressed a kiss to the top of her head. The idea that she'd marry someone old enough to be her grandfather made Malcolm see red. What he wouldn't give to find the duke still in the card room. He'd storm in there and demand satisfaction from her grandfather. Then, he'd promise to haunt him until he agreed to allow Celeste to marry him.

"It's a price I am willing to pay for what I want." She kissed the middle of his chest where his heart resided. "Now, I've become greedy. Not only do I want my mother and grandfather to make amends to one another and the mortgage forgiven, but I want to experience pleasure and desire with a man that makes my…"

"That makes your what?" he asked as he tilted her chin

to see the emotion in her eyes. Where he expected to see sadness or even a bit of melancholy, he saw something that looked more like desire mixed with fortitude and determination.

Celeste Worsley was certainly not a mild or meek woman who let others make decisions for her. She went after what she wanted, no matter the sacrifice.

"I want to experience pleasure with someone who makes my heart pound and draws my every attention just because he's in the room." She smiled shyly. "More of the type of pleasure that we shared at the wedding breakfast and when we kissed. Alice told me that her entire body thrums in anticipation when she's with Benjamin." She bit her lower lip, then soothed it with her tongue.

Malcolm barely contained a groan as his entire body tightened at the sight. His cock twitched, and he felt himself getting harder by the second just by looking at her and those plump, lush lips that deserved to be savored and worshipped by him. He blew out a breath but didn't answer her.

She tilted her head until her brilliant eyes locked with his. "That's what I want. And I want it with you."

Malcolm had always considered himself an honorable man who would never ruin a woman. But the siren standing before him made him want to toss every piece of integrity and principle he possessed out the window.

She was an innocent, not to mention a duke's granddaughter.

"Malcolm," she whispered in that honeyed voice that made him crave more of her delicious kisses. "I know what I am asking of you. Don't make me beg."

He tilted his head to the sky and gazed at the stars. However, he didn't see any of it. Her voice and her eyes were dispatched from another world, one that promised heaven. That's why she was named Celeste. The heavens sent her to torment him tonight. What she wanted would make a saint sin without regret. Malcolm might be noble in character, but he was a man after all, and the woman standing before him made him want to throw all caution to the wind.

She reminded him of the forbidden fruit. She'd taste so sweet, but the ramifications afterward would be too great a price for both of them. He couldn't forget Alice and Benjamin. Their indiscretion had resulted in a baby. Though their marriage had protected them, that was not the case for Celeste's parents. If he and Celeste were caught, they'd have to marry. Truthfully, that was what he wanted. But he didn't want Celeste to be forced to marry him. It had to be her own decision. He would never jeopardize Celeste's virtue and reputation that way.

She was Exehill's beloved granddaughter. Malcolm had asked Pelham to help him impress the old man. Well, he'd certainly be the exact opposite of impressed if he discovered that Malcolm had had his wicked way with his granddaughter.

He studied her expression, and the truth couldn't be denied. Celeste wanted him. She stood before him now, making him an offer he should refuse in good conscience. He'd tried to be a man of good repute who had the respect of his peers. And frankly, that hadn't gotten him very far in his quest for a wife. Perhaps it was time to change tactics.

"If I agree, then I have two conditions."

A fine line appeared between her brows as she considered what he'd said. "Go on."

"You will suspend your efforts to find me a wife." He leaned close and inhaled her sweet rose scent. "My scruples will not allow me to share my lips, my embraces, or anything else with you while trying to win the favor of another woman."

Her eyes widened at his candor. "I wouldn't want to cause you any harm. It's an excellent thought. I must be honest. I wouldn't be jealous of seeing you with another." She swallowed, and the slight movement of her throat drove him mad. "I agree."

He wanted to point out that, as his wife, she would never suffer any jealousy. He would be completely committed to her. What was he saying? He was getting ahead of himself. She wanted pleasure, and he was thinking of marriage.

"I'll help you experience pleasure, but we will not make love. You are my greatest weakness and desire, but I can't offer more. You're not mine...yet. I have to protect your reputation and mine, duchess. That means you and I —" He couldn't finish the thought as she smashed her mouth to his. Her low moan vibrated against his chest. He wrapped her in his arms and licked her bottom lip. Instead of allowing him to deepen the kiss, she pulled away.

Her eyes searched his as a smile grew brighter than the full moon's glow behind her. "That means you and I shall become excellent friends."

He laughed. "You are a clever girl." All he wanted was to press his lips where her pulse pounded at the base of her neck. It would be as sweet and soft as he'd imagined. "It also means that we're together."

She nodded slightly. "Until we aren't."

Little did Celeste know that he was determined that those words would never be spoken between them. He planned to do everything in his power to make her want to be his. He wanted her to fall in love with him.

"When shall we start?" she asked.

"This moment," he murmured, taking her mouth with his.

Celeste's heart threatened to break through her chest. This was what she had wanted, dreamed about but never thought she'd have. But here she was in the garden with Malcolm Hollandale kissing her with a reverence that threatened to steal her breath.

His lips brushed against hers. She wrapped her arms around his neck and threaded her fingers through his soft blond locks. When she groaned her pleasure at the fleeting touch, he chuckled low, then pressed his lips against hers.

He licked her bottom lip, then pulled away slightly. "Patience, darling. All good things come to those who wait."

"But I've waited so long," she pouted. When he pulled away and studied her, she didn't shy away. "I have a confession. Did you know I've wanted you since the very first time I saw you?"

His brow furrowed at her words.

But she didn't let it deter her from telling him the truth. "I think I've been infatuated with you since that first day." She nipped his bottom lip, tempting him to kiss her again. She slipped off her gloves and let them fall to the ground. She wanted her skin against his with no barriers between them. "Every single day since Lord and Lady Lowndes' ball last spring."

He rested his forehead against hers as he took a shuddering breath, then grinned mischievously. "I shall never live with myself if I disappoint you."

She laughed softly. "You would never disappoint me. How could you when this is all I've ever thought about?"

Like lightning, he pulled her close again, never taking his eyes away from hers. Only when he pressed his lips against hers did his eyes close. "Duchess," he murmured against his lips as he tenderly caressed the softness of her cheeks.

She opened her mouth, and his tongue slid past her lips, tasting, lingering, exploring every inch of her. They were equals, taking their time as they allowed the passion to ignite between them. Her legs trembled as their tongues danced against each other. Unable to stand it, she pushed her body closer and rubbed her breasts against his chest. They'd grown tender and heavy. The urge to get closer and anchor herself to him became relentless.

He groaned his approval as his hands cupped her bottom and brought her close. His erection felt like forged steel against her softness. He canted his hips and ground against her.

"Please," she whimpered.

He slowly ran his hands over her ribs and cupped her breasts. She mewled with pleasure. Everything inside of her turned to molten heat.

Still holding her close, he traced a finger around her bodice. "I want to kiss you here." He squeezed her breast.

She arched her back, offering herself to him. His lips skimmed a path up her neck as his clever hand found a way to free one of her breasts. The cool air hitting her skin did nothing to quench the heat that roared through her. When he pinched her nipple, her knees buckled. But the hand around her waist tightened to keep her from falling into a heap. The brief hint of pain swiftly transformed into a sensation she'd never experienced. Pleasure pulsed through every inch of her.

He nipped at the tender skin below her ear, then laved it with his tongue. She tilted her neck, giving him greater access as she pushed her center into his hardness, begging for relief.

"That's it, darling. Rub against me. Find your pleasure," he murmured, then bit her ear lobe.

Wild with need, she was ready to beg him for more, but she didn't need to. Malcolm bent his head and kissed the top of her breast, then circled his tongue around the darkened skin surrounding her nipple. It was glorious but not enough.

"Please, Malcolm," she whimpered.

As soon as the words were out of her mouth, he sucked her nipple, then licked it with his tongue.

Her toes curled at the pleasure he'd summoned with such an act. She clenched her legs as her wetness grew. Good God, she could feel her arousal on her thighs. She moaned as she imagined him trailing his fingers against her folds, then sweeping his finger through them until he found the tender nub.

"You taste like heaven. If we were someplace private, I'd dispatch your dress and stays to feast upon every inch of you."

She groaned again and pulled his hair, urging him to continue his ministrations.

"Would you like that?"

She whimpered her answer as she sought to relieve the pressure building inside her. Without considering how wanton she must appear, she took one of his hands and pressed it to her center, where it ached.

"What do you want?" he growled as he continued to kiss her tender flesh.

"Touch me."

His hand skated over her hip as he slowly raised her

gown. "If I touched you where you ache, what would I find?" His lips touched hers. "Are you wet for me?"

She clenched her center as she summoned every ounce of courage to answer.

"Say it," he commanded, then licked her lips.

Whenever she was in bed, in the late hours, she thought of him. When she grew hot and achy, it was always him that caused her to become aroused. Fantasy was nowhere near as thrilling as real life.

"Yes."

"I want to hear the words from your lips, Celeste. I'll keep them forever. Now, say it. For me."

She whimpered, unable to deny him. "I'm wet."

"For me," he demanded softly. "Say it."

"For you. I'm wet for you. Only you."

He growled softly. "Good."

He kissed her as if she were the very breath he needed. All the while, he was drawing circles on her thighs. Her damn stockings were the only thing that kept him from touching her skin. The man was a virtuoso who played her like a fine instrument, building sensation upon sensation. She'd never been so aroused and needy in her life.

"All right, love," he whispered against her lips. He was panting as if he'd run a race. They were both lost in their own world where sensation, touch, and heat were the only things that mattered.

She widened her stance slightly and silently begged him to touch her where no hand but hers had touched before. When his fingers skated on her bare skin, she inhaled sharply.

At her moan, he inhaled deeply. "I can smell your arousal. God, I'd give anything to taste you right now. I want to lick every bit of your sweetness until you come against my mouth."

She cried out when his fingers caressed her slick folds. Unable to resist, she pushed against his hand.

"Darling, hush," he murmured, then chuckled. "I promise to take care of you." As his fingers found her tender nub, he said, "You're swollen and wet. For me. Only me."

"Yes," she whispered. "It's all for you." Her breathlessness surprised her. She'd never felt this urgency before, even when she pleasured herself.

He slid his finger around her most sensitive spot, taunting and teasing her. Every third circle or so, he pressed against her clitoris. She sucked in a breath. Pleasure swirled throughout her body. She had brought herself to orgasm with her own hand, but having Malcolm touch her was incomparable. The tenderness of his attention and the press of his lips against her mouth was almost too much.

"You are so precious to me," he whispered. He canted his hips, pushing his hard cock against her center.

Unable to help herself, she wrapped a leg around his, determined to get closer to him. Needing to get closer. He was like the air that she breathed. Essential and life-affirming. She wanted him to fill every empty space within her and never let go.

He took her in a punishing kiss that threatened to steal her very essence. At this point, she didn't care. She'd give him everything and not ask for anything in return as long as he continued to touch her as if he worshipped her.

Celeste held her breath as the sensation built. Suddenly, it became too much. She closed her eyes as weightlessness overtook her body as if she were soaring through the sky.

Malcolm, I'm…"

"Let go," he whispered. "I have you."

Unleashed, her orgasm wrapped around her, cocooning her in an indescribable pleasure. It was like heaven had fallen to earth and landed on her body.

"Malcolm," she cried softly as she grabbed one of his lapels and held on for dear life.

A moan rose from behind them.

Suddenly, Malcolm pulled her behind him but held onto her hand. "Who's there?"

Instantly, Celeste put herself to rights. For the love of heaven, someone was nearby.

In one quick movement, Malcolm picked up her gloves and then pulled her into the shadows where the moonlight couldn't reach them. He gently pushed her against one of the stone walls and covered her with his body, shielding her from any prying eyes. He brought his mouth to her ear. "Celeste," he whispered as if he were in pain. "I have to get you back to the ballroom. There's a couple on the terrace. They might have seen or heard us."

She nodded but held on to him. Her entire body still tingled as he embraced her, then rested his forehead against hers.

Soft murmurs sounded in the garden before they grew silent.

"Please hold me," she whispered. She clung to him, not wanting to let go as the severity of their situation crowded into her thoughts.

"It would kill me if I did anything to hurt you." He tucked her close and locked his gaze with hers. "If I harmed your reputation—"

She pressed her lips to his. "Hush. You have nothing to apologize for."

She rested her head against his chest and breathed in his sandalwood scent. The pounding of her heart matched his. He was always so sure of himself, but the thought that he worried about her touched her deep inside. How many people in her life were concerned about her the way that he was? The more time she spent around Malcolm Hollandale, the more she understood that he would think of her needs before his.

She cupped his cheek. "I should be the one concerned about your reputation. Thank you for thinking of me."

"Always." Reverently, he pressed a kiss to her palm. "I need to get you safely inside. But I will never forget this night." He pulled back and gazed at her. "It was the first time I held Celeste Worsley as she fell apart in my arms." He pressed his lips against hers again. "It won't be the last. I think I've become addicted to you, duchess."

She smiled as she pressed her lips against his. "It's unfair. I didn't get to pleasure you." She glanced at the bulge in his breeches where his erection still stood in prominence. If anyone saw him in such a state, they'd know exactly what he'd been doing, and they wouldn't have trouble guessing who he'd been with.

She waved a hand in the direction of his engorged cock. "Is there anything I can do to help you with…that?" Heat bludgeoned her cheeks at such an audacious suggestion.

"I think tonight should only be about you." His tender smile made her heart skip a beat. "You've already helped me enough."

"How could I if you're…still like that?" She refused to allow her inexperience to taint what they'd shared here. "Perhaps, we could continue, and I can touch you like you touched me." She studied, but in the dark shadows, it wasn't easy to see his expression. Perhaps he was anxious to be rid of her. "Unless you'd like to return to the ballroom posthaste." She straightened her stance and took a deep breath. "I would understand."

He growled, then took her in another punishing kiss. "Well, I wouldn't understand. All I want is to hold you all night and kiss you until the lark sings." He looked toward the house, but they couldn't see anything because of the walls. "I wouldn't care if Lady Ravenscroft was the one who found us."

"Malcolm," she scolded playfully. "She would be horrified. Even though you're a silver-tongued devil, I'm not certain you could talk your way out of such a scathing scandal."

A lopsided grin tugged at one side of his mouth. "She loves the theatre almost as much as you. I'd offer her my box for the next opening night."

Her breath caught at the words. "You're not going to attend?"

"Of course, I am." He cupped her cheeks once again. "You're going to be there, correct?" When she nodded, he continued, "Then I'll be there." He winked at her, then pressed a light kiss to her nose. "I'm finding that my social calendar revolves around you now." He pulled away and took her hand. "Come, my little siren."

Embolden, she stood on her tiptoes and pressed a light kiss to his cheek. "Do you like having your social calendar coincide with mine?"

He rested his forehead against hers and drew a deep breath. "I've discovered it's my favorite thing in the world."

CHAPTER NINE

"This is what your mother gave up when she decided to elope with that man," Celeste's grandfather murmured loud enough that the Duke of Pelham grimaced.

They'd just arrived for the duke's dinner party, and already, Celeste wanted to hide. Fire licked her cheeks at her grandfather's audacity to even mention her parents in such a negative manner in front of the Duke of Pelham.

"She gave up prestige and respect—"

Pelham thankfully interrupted her grandfather's next diatribe. "Exehill, the other guests have arrived and are waiting for us in the salon." Pelham smiled benevolently at Celeste and extended his arm. "Come, Miss Worsley. My sisters are anxious to see you again."

"And I as well. I saw Lady Honoria at Lord Raven-scroft's ball. It was the first time I've seen her since finishing school." Celeste wrapped her arm around his. "But I do keep up my acquaintance with Lady Pippa."

"Honoria doesn't care for London like Pippa and I do. I consider myself fortunate to have both of them with me this time." The duke led her and her grandfather through the massive entry at Ardeerton House, his London home. With daffodil-colored walls and flooring in black and white marble tiles, the airy entry could easily host a small ball. Celeste tried not to gawk, but it was impossible. A marble statue of a reclining Mars gazed south, while a matching statue of Venus looked north. Separated by an entire room, their fervent gazes focused solely on one another. They appeared to be making love with their watchful eyes.

Pelham nodded at something her grandfather had said, then leaned close. "Impressive, are they not?"

"Indeed, Your Grace," she replied. "I can't quit staring at them."

"I'll let you in on a little secret. Sometimes in the morning, I have my tea here. It's just me, Mars, and Venus. No one else. It's peaceful and allows me to reflect on what I must accomplish that day. But when the sunrise hits their faces, it almost appears they're conversing with one another." He winked. "Of course, I try not to interrupt."

Before she could ask more, they were in the formal salon.

Everyone turned in their direction. It seemed all of London's elite were attending the duke's dinner party. Lord Ravenscroft, Lord Trafford, Lord Wade, Mr. Carter Dodd, and Mr. Damien DeWitt were in attendance. Celeste nodded with a smile as she caught the attention of Lady Mercy and Lady Giselle. Yet, as she continued to glance about the room, she sighed silently. Malcolm wasn't there.

Not forgetting her manners, she smiled when the Duke of Pelham's sisters approached. Blonde, tall in stature, and possessing striking blue eyes, they resembled their handsome brother.

The duke smiled affectionately as they came to his side.

"Welcome to Ardeerton House." Honoria didn't stand on ceremony as she hugged Celeste.

"Thank you." Celeste returned the hug.

Pippa embraced her next with a massive smile on her face. "Celeste, welcome."

"Thank you for inviting me and my grandfather."

By then, her grandfather's laughter echoed around the room as he greeted several of his cronies. For the first time since they'd arrived, Celeste breathed easier. Perhaps her grandfather would forget about her parents for one evening.

Lady Honoria beamed. "This is Pelham's first dinner party at Ardeerton House since Pippa and I arrived in London." She squeezed Celeste's arm. "Having you here makes it even more memorable."

"I do hope we get a chance to share each other's news this evening." Celeste waved a hand. "Not that I have any worth sharing."

What a bouncer. Besides the fact that her longtime friend and lady's maid was married and carrying, and her grandfather still harbored a grudge against her mother. Not to mention, Celeste had done *unspeakable but oh-so-pleasurable things* in Mr. Malcolm Hollandale's arms several nights ago while they were in Lord Ravenscroft's courtyard.

"Didn't I see you dance with Mr. Hollandale?" Honoria asked, then smiled. "You two seemed quite taken with each other in the courtyard."

Suddenly, she was unable to speak. If Lady Honoria saw her with Malcolm, then who else had?

Lady Honoria frowned. "I didn't mean to upset you. Lord Trafford and I were in the courtyard enjoying the fresh air. Lots of couples were there. Don't be alarmed."

She patted Celeste's hand and offered her a comforting smile.

Celeste shook her head slightly. If her grandfather had an inkling what she'd done, he'd banish Celeste to her parents' home with an edict never to appear in his sight again. The mortgage would probably come due the next day.

She should be more worried. But her situation was becoming clearer as the days wore on. Her grandfather was using her to further his wealth by marrying her to the man of his choosing. She would secure her family's future and hopefully, heal the wounds that tore them apart.

She cleared her throat slightly. What was the matter with her? To even contemplate such unkind thoughts made her as much of a manipulator as her grandfather.

Her beloved mother had never once uttered an unkind word about her grandfather. Her father hadn't either. But sometimes, when he pursed his lips, it was easy to see how angry her father was at her grandfather. But her father loved her mother and had always tried to make her happy. Celeste knew that she was fortunate to have parents who loved each other, and they loved her.

Growing up, she would ask why they never saw her grandfather. Her mother said he was an important and busy man in London. The only time Celeste ever heard from him was when he sent her letters wishing her birthday was a happy day. Then he'd called her to London, and her mother and father's relief was palpable that she would have a Season.

It wasn't until she stayed with her grandfather that she understood the depth of his rancor.

"Miss Worsley, there you are." Malcolm's whisky-dark baritone surrounded her.

Caught off-guard, she shivered slightly. He'd used the

same voice the night he kissed her senseless as he brought her pleasure.

"Lady Honoria." He bowed to both of them.

"I'm glad you could attend, Mr. Hollandale." Honoria smiled, then briefly turned her gaze to the crowd. " If you both will excuse me. Pippa is motioning for me."

After Honoria left, Celeste tipped her gaze to his. For a moment, the rest of the crowd fell away, and the earth seemed to still on its axis. Malcolm stood before her with a secret smile that promised all sorts of pleasure.

"Mr. Hollandale," she murmured. "I hope you have been well."

"How you say my name invokes all sorts of images in my mind." He bowed slightly, then whispered seductively. "All of them are of you naked in my bed."

Celeste bent her head to hide her instant blush. His eyes blazed brighter than the midday sun when she lifted her gaze. He was as affected as she was by their physical attraction to one another.

The crowd grew louder as the Duke of Pelham escorted Lord Ravenscroft's mother into the dining room. Her grandfather followed, escorting Lady Pippa. Lord Trafford held Lady Honoria's arm. Celeste relaxed when it became clear that the Duke of Pelham was not following the orders of precedence. She glanced at her grandfather, who didn't seem to notice, or if he did, he didn't care.

"May I escort you in?" Malcolm moved closer, offering his arm. His familiar fragrance enveloped her like an embrace.

"Please." For a moment, she didn't recognize her voice for the tremulousness in it.

"That's what you said to me repeatedly that night," he teased softly.

Celeste slightly pinched his arm. "You did the same."

"You wound me, Miss Worsley," Malcolm drawled with a smile.

By then, they were in the formal dining room where the longest table Celeste had ever seen stood center. Footmen were pouring wine and placing small trays of food upon the table.

Malcolm escorted her to her chair and then sat next to her. Celeste grinned but immediately bit her lip so no one would see how pleased she was with her dinner companion. However, she murmured for Malcolm's ears alone, "How fortuitous that I'm seated next to you."

Malcolm unfolded his serviette and then placed it in his lap. With no warning, his leg brushed against hers, then stayed there. She didn't move, but she clenched every muscle to keep from making a fool of herself by turning his way and demanding a kiss.

"I've missed you," he whispered with a smile.

"The same for me," she confided. By then, the footmen were serving a clear consommé. The soup course was followed by lobster and fried parsley. As everyone ate, Celeste could hardly take a bite. She could feel Malcolm's heat surrounding her. Yet, she shivered at his nearness. Every time his gaze met hers, it felt like his fingers stroked her body with the same tenderness he'd pleasured her with that night.

She forced her gaze to his and let out a breath. He was addressing Lady Pippa, who sat on his other side. Her grandfather sat across from Malcolm and appeared to be watching him much like a hawk studied its prey before striking.

Celeste turned her gaze in the other direction. The guests in attendance included Mr. Carter Dodd and Lady Mercy Ainsworth, who was attending with her father. Mr. Damien DeWitt was also in attendance, along with Miss

Lucy Montgomery and Lord Wade. Celeste had seen them all numerous times at various social events, including the theatre. But tonight, it seemed as if they were more jovial than usual. Undoubtedly, they were thrilled that the Duke of Pelham had included them tonight. Yet, Celeste didn't have a chance to feel such joy. She felt ready to explode. Without looking at Malcolm, she knew every minuscule move he made. That's how aware of him she was.

What if she did explode and caused a scene? She, more than anyone else, knew that her grandfather would disapprove of any display of emotion from her.

He wanted her calm and collected, much like a child's doll. He took her out to admire and show her to others, but his attention never lasted. When he grew bored, he put her away until he needed her, then he'd take her out again.

"Miss Worsley?"

A male voice drew her attention from her musings.

"Your parents are friends of mine from long ago. I purchased a racehorse from your father's stables. How are they?" asked Lord Ravenscroft, who sat diagonally across from her.

Celeste held her serviette to her mouth, then slowly settled it back on her lap. During a formal dinner party, one was only allowed to converse with the guest to the left and right. That was not the case with the Duke of Pelham. He was an unconventional duke who apparently didn't care for meaningless rules. Proof in point was that the duke owned a gambling hell adjacent to his ducal seat in Amesbury.

Not only did her grandfather not approve of gambling, but Celeste would wager that he didn't care for Lord Ravenscroft's questions about her mother and father either.

She wore her best smile and turned to the marquess.

"They are very well, my lord. I shall tell them that you inquired after their health and happiness."

"Lovely people." Lord Ravenscroft nodded his head and smiled. "Does your father still have an impressive stable? I bought my racehorse, Hempleworth, from him." He turned to some of the other guests. "People come from all over England to purchase his horseflesh. He has excellent stock."

"He's a simple horse breeder," her grandfather murmured to no one, but Celeste knew it was directed toward her.

She didn't glance his way as she adjusted her silverware, then turned her attention back to the marquess. She would defy her grandfather by continuing the conversation. She never had the courage before, but she'd changed since last week. She was stronger and knew what she wanted. Malcolm taught her there was nothing wrong with thinking about yourself. Right now, she wanted to honor her father even if it infuriated her grandfather.

"He does, sir. I'm certain you'd be welcome to visit."

Before she could say anymore, a spoon clattered onto an empty plate. A few feminine gasps sounded around the table. Celeste didn't have to look in the direction of the sound to determine who had dropped their spoon. It was her grandfather. He was letting everyone know that he was tired of the conversation.

"Thankfully, my granddaughter is nothing like her parents," her grandfather said aloud.

Her cheeks heated as she stared at her plate. When she lifted her head, Malcolm caught her gaze. Fury blazed in his blue eyes.

Without anyone knowing, he placed his hand on her thigh and squeezed gently, offering her comfort. Celeste placed her hand over his hoping he understood how much she appreciated his kindness. He flipped his hand over and threaded their fingers together. They stayed like that until the footmen served the next course.

Pelham glanced in their direction and lifted an eyebrow. Malcolm nodded discreetly.

"Exehill," Pelham drawled. "You really should come to the Jolly Rooster. I'll ensure that you have the finest accommodations." The duke pointed at Lord Trafford. "He bought an estate not far from mine. He's running a foundation for young peers who've lost their parents."

Trafford nodded. "Indeed, we always need mentors, especially dukes, to help with the young charges." He smiled at her. "Miss Worsley, you're welcome as well."

"Thank you," she said demurely.

"Hollandale visits regularly," Lord Trafford offered. "He's very generous with his time and money."

"Thank you." Malcolm nodded toward the earl.

Ravenscroft leaned back in his chair. "Hollandale visits on occasion when the millionaires have a meeting at the Jolly Rooster."

Malcolm nodded with a smile. "I do, but I won't wager unless it's a sure bet."

Her grandfather narrowed his eyes and glared at Malcolm. "You're a member of Pelham's Millionaires Club?"

Before Malcolm could answer, Pelham did the honors for him. "He was the fourth member. Made a fortune from glazes for tiles and greenware. His product is used all over the world."

"Impressive," her grandfather commented with a smile.

Practically giddy at her grandfather's response, Celeste smiled at Malcolm. Perhaps her grandfather would see how marvelous he was.

Trafford smiled at Honoria, then turned his attention to

her grandfather. "Hollandale took the top marks in chemistry, science, and mathematics at Eton."

"Don't forget physics," someone from the other end of the table reminded him.

Celeste tightened her stomach when her grandfather leaned back in his chair and placed an elbow on the arm. It made him look relaxed and good-humored. But she knew that pose intimately. He'd done it to her a thousand times, waiting to attack her or her parents over some indiscretion.

"Who are your people?" Her grandfather wore a ghost of a smile.

Pelham rolled his eyes at the question. Lord Ravenscroft and Lord Trafford fixed their gazes on her grandfather. They were being incredibly supportive of the man sitting next to her. Malcolm Hollandale was the most gifted, generous, handsome, not to mention desirable man she had the good fortune to meet.

But Malcolm didn't seem bothered by the attention. "My father is the vicar of a small parish in Wiltshire. Before that, he worked at the parish in Amesbury."

"How did someone like you become admitted to Eton? Is your family wealthy?"

Her grandfather was like a dog fighting over a bone. Uncomfortable with his questions, she squirmed slightly in her seat.

"His father was my tutor," Pelham practically growled the words. "Hollandale takes after his father. He's brilliant."

Malcolm lifted his hand in Pelham's direction. "Thank you, my friend, for the kind words, but I should answer His Grace's question." Malcolm turned his gaze to her grandfather. "My father's income did not allow for such an expense. I had a benefactor who paid for my tuition to Eton."

"How fortunate for you, Mr. Hollandale," her grandfather replied. But then he tilted his head as if regarding Malcolm as some strange creature he'd never seen before. "Amazing that a man in trade such as yourself is welcome in the rarified company of so many men your superior."

Celeste couldn't breathe. She could only stare at her grandfather. Finally, she took in a deep breath. "Grandfather, Mr. Hollandale is more than a man of trade, I assure you."

Then he turned his attention to Celeste like a raptor when it saw better prey to focus his hunt on. "You assure me, do you? Is this the same Malcolm Hollandale who hired your lady's maid right out from under me?" His gaze whipped to Malcolm. "Why, pray tell, do you need a lady's maid in your employment?"

Malcolm calmly pushed his dinner plate away but never turned his gaze from her grandfather. "Your Grace, I have two residences. One in Mayfair and one on Church Street. I've needed servants in the Church Street residence for quite a while. Miss Alice Cummings interviewed for employment, and my secretary found her qualified." He quickly turned to Celeste. "I am dreadfully sorry that you lost your lady's maid."

"She's a wonderful employee, and I'm sure you'll be pleased with her work," Celeste said quietly.

Thankfully, it was the end of the meal, and footmen were clearing the table. Before anyone could say another word, Honoria spoke. "Ladies, shall we leave the table? I think it's time for us to depart for tea and other refreshments." She'd pushed her chair back to stand when her grandfather raised his hand.

"If I may have one more minute, Lady Honoria. I have some wonderful news I'd like to share with everyone here tonight." Her grandfather didn't look at her. Instead, he stared straight at Malcolm. "It's my pleasure to announce that my granddaughter is betrothed to the Marquess of Grolier, the heir to the Duke of Wilkes-Hare.

No. He did not say those words. But she was proven wrong as his voice echoed around the room. Celeste didn't move or breathe. Her ears rang, and her eyes blurred. For a moment, she'd thought she'd faint. Her body seemed to float above the table, watching but not participating in this nightmare of a dinner party.

Malcolm didn't say a word. Several others murmured their felicitations, but Celeste didn't acknowledge them. All she could manage were three words that she whispered to Malcolm.

"I didn't know."

Malcolm didn't acknowledge her. Instead, he placed his hands on the table and slowly stood. His gaze was locked on her grandfather, who leaned back in his chair and rested his elbows on the chair arms. Then to ice the proverbial cake, he steepled his fingers. He let everyone know that he was quite pleased with himself.

Honoria stood, and the other ladies followed. Celeste was the last to leave the formal dining room. As the others chattered about the upcoming Season, several ladies wished her congratulations.

All Celeste could do was nod her head. Her grandfather had never told her that he'd picked out someone for her to marry. She'd never even met the man. She had no idea who the Marquess of Grolier was or where he lived.

Suddenly, she felt nauseous. She slowed as the ladies headed to the music room where the tea service was being laid out.

She ducked into a small card room, then walked to the tall windows overlooking the duke's courtyard and rested her heated brow against the cool glass.

For the love of heaven, she had to talk to Malcolm and explain...what? Even she didn't understand what had happened in the dining room. Her grandfather had attacked Malcolm, then her, before blasting her entire world asunder. He picked out a bridegroom without even discussing it with her.

But that's what she had agreed to—a simple bargain with the devil so her parents would again be welcomed in London and debt-free. Her eyes burned and her throat tightened as a single tear fell.

The deal she'd struck did little to alleviate her feeling that she'd betrayed not only Malcolm but also herself.

CHAPTER TEN

Malcolm rose from the table and walked to the nearest footman, who held a tray filled with glasses of port, whisky, and brandy. Without a word, Malcolm took a whisky and swallowed it in one gulp.

A perfect night had turned into a nightmare. And Celeste hadn't said a word to him. When they'd touched under the table, it seemed as if they were in their own world where no one would intrude. Perhaps he'd been the only one who believed in that enchantment.

Pelham came to his side and clapped him gently on the shoulder. "Go find her. If she's with the other ladies, send my butler into the room and ask her to follow him."

Malcolm just stared at him as if he were speaking another language. "Why would I do that?"

Pelham lifted a perfectly arched blond brow and regarded him. "You couldn't see her face, but Celeste was as shocked as you were by that betrothal announcement."

"Who is the Marquess of Grolier?" Malcolm growled in a low voice. Just saying the name made him want to pound his fist into a wall.

"I've heard the name but never met him." The duke glanced over his shoulder for a moment. "I'll ask Ravenscroft's mother. She studies Debrett's Peerage religiously. Her aunt is well-connected in society. If anyone has information, Lady Ravenscroft will."

Malcolm glanced at the Duke of Exehill. "I swear the man is baiting me. He knows I have an interest in his granddaughter."

Pelham nodded. "It looked like more than an interest tonight, my friend." When Malcolm narrowed his eyes, Pelham lifted a brow. "Go. I'll keep the old goat entertained and ask him about Grolier while you find out what happened with your Celeste."

Malcolm wanted to roar, but instead, he nodded at his friend and then placed his empty glass on the table. Inconspicuously, he left the dining room and started down the hall.

What should he say to her? Did she know the man? When were they to marry? She'd been truthful about her expectations. He was a fool, a damn fool, to believe he could change her mind.

The door of the music room was ajar. Conversations floated in the air, but there was no hint of Celeste's voice.

Celeste was the definition of a celestial being who had come into his orbit then blown his world to pieces. Her betrothal announcement reminded him of the disappointment he experienced when one of his experiments failed. Only tonight, the pain felt like he'd been stabbed in the gut.

The card room's door was open. All the other rooms down the hallway were closed. He took a chance and entered. Celeste stood, staring out the windows. Quietly, he closed the door. She was lost in another world with her arms wrapped around her waist as if she were protecting herself.

The sight of tears on her cheek undid him. Her grandfather had hurt her without a care. Celeste was the duke's flesh and blood, and he ignored her as if she were dirt beneath his feet instead of treating her as a prized jewel he should have been proud of.

Malcolm cursed under his breath as he strode to her side. He wrapped his arms around her.

She turned in his embrace and buried her head against his chest. "I didn't know. I swear to you, I didn't know."

"I know, darling." God, he would tear the old man apart with his bare hands for what he had done to her. She was heartbroken. "I didn't see your face, but Pelham told me you were just as shocked as I was."

She clasped his lapels in her hands and slowly lifted her tear-stained face until she could meet his gaze. "I'm sorry. I'm so, so sorry."

"Don't apologize, duchess. It's not your fault," he soothed. He pulled away and grasped her shoulders. "Do you know the man?"

"I've never met him." Her voice had turned eerily tremulous as if she were barely holding on to her emotions.

He took her handkerchief out of his pocket, then wiped her eyes.

She smiled weakly. "Is that my handkerchief?"

He nodded, then squeezed her shoulders. "I carry it with me everywhere. It's like I have a piece of you near my heart."

How could her grandfather give her to someone she'd never met? It was as if Exehill still believed in the medieval custom of people marrying sight unseen, allying families so they wouldn't declare war on one another.

He kissed her forehead tenderly and then stared into her eyes. He had to know the truth no matter how much it destroyed him. "Do you want to marry him?"

She let out a sad, soulful sigh, then shook her head. "Not now. Not after my time with you."

Every muscle relaxed and he tugged her into his arms and held her. If she didn't want to marry the man, he'd do everything in his power to ensure that she wasn't forced to. He'd give his fortune to the bastard if it would save Celeste from this marriage.

"What am I going to do?" Her voice faded as if she were talking to herself. "I promised my grandfather I'd marry the man he chose for me."

He kissed the top of her head, then captured her gaze. "You're not marrying the Marquess of Grolier. You and I will think of something."

"I don't even know his name." She pulled away and returned to her study out the window. "Malcolm, my parents cannot reconcile with him unless I do as he says. They'll never be able to pay off that mortgage."

He narrowed the distance between them, took her hands in his, and pulled her to face him. "Celeste, did you hear what he said at dinner? His animosity toward your parents, particularly your mother, was fully displayed tonight. By attacking your parents, he is, in essence, attacking you. Why should you sacrifice yourself in a marriage that will only benefit your grandfather? He will not forgive your family's debt. Nor does your grandfather intend to heal the rift between your parents and him."

She bit her lower lip. The urge to press his lips to hers became almost unbearable. But kisses and caresses had to wait. He would fix this for her. Somehow. Someway.

She straightened her spine. "If there's talk of a special license, I'll claim I must visit my parents first." She fisted her hand. "Or I'll tell him he must invite them to town before I marry."

"That's my duchess." Whatever shock Celeste had felt earlier was diminishing. She was starting to take control of her life once more. It was one of her most admirable traits, in his opinion. When she'd walked into Drury Lane, she was a woman who would not be defeated. Tonight, she was showing that same strength.

He took her hand and pressed his lips to it. "Pelham is trying to discover who Grolier is and where he's from. I'll speak with Lady Ravenscroft as she's an expert on Debrett's Peerage." He smiled against her kidskin glove. "Who would have ever thought that I would care what was in the pages of that book?"

"Would you believe that I memorized the *bloody* thing?"

He smiled at the curse that tripped from her sweet lips.

"I never once came across a title with Grolier in it." Her shoulders drooped. "I've wasted so much time in my life already." She smiled and squeezed his hand. "Trying to win my grandfather's affection. Trying to make amends for my parents, who I'm quickly learning are not at fault for the estrangement with my grandfather. Hours memorizing Debrett's. But do you know what I most regret?"

Malcolm shook his head as he continued to hold her hand to his mouth. The slight shake of his head allowed him to caress and cherish her. Never in his life had he thought he'd find someone like Celeste. And he'd be damned if he'd lose her to another man, particularly someone she didn't even want.

"I regret not telling you how long I've been infatuated with you. I have been since I first saw you and didn't know your name." She chuckled softly. "You weren't in

Debrett's, and that should have been my first clue that I was wasting my time studying such worthless pages."

She stood on tiptoes and placed a tender kiss against his mouth. He marveled at the softness of her lush lips against his. She'd hidden her feelings for him for ages, and he never knew.

"Why did you always appear aloof?"

She shook her head. "Would you believe that I was a bit timid around you. I was concerned that you'd think that I was just an insipid woman chasing after you."

"Celeste," he countered with a frown. "No one chased after me. I've been trying desperately to find a wife, and no one would give me a second look."

"Not to your face. But hordes of women stare at you when they don't think others are watching. You're handsome, rich, and have a body fashioned for a woman's pleasure. I should know. I was one of those women."

"Well, you're the only one I want to share my body with now."

When she blushed, he wrapped his arms around her and kissed her slowly and reverently. He gripped her tighter as he deepened the kiss, letting her know how much he wanted her. This was the way that they would always be together, their smoldering passion ready to alight into a desire neither could ignore.

Her grandfather's voice echoed down the hall. "Where is that girl? It's time to leave."

She broke the kiss and murmured, "I must go."

"When will I see you again?" he said, not caring that he sounded desperate. The idea that she would be in her grandfather's company was worrisome. "I don't want you to go with him."

Celeste placed her hand on his lips. "Nothing will

happen this evening. I'll send a note where and when we can meet."

Before he could answer, she pressed her lips against his, then exited the room without a goodbye.

Her grandfather's voice called out her name. "Celeste, where have you been, girl? You should never keep me waiting."

Malcolm fisted his hand to keep himself from confronting the duke, then railing at him. For the love of heaven, it took every ounce of restraint he possessed not to go after her.

He couldn't lose her. It would be as if he'd had his own heart ripped from his chest.

He closed his eyes as the truth slowly seeped into his thoughts. He loved her.

He had lost his heart to Miss Celeste Worsley. Malcolm didn't know when it had happened, but he had no doubt that his heart was hers forever.

And he'd be damned if he would allow another man to claim his duchess.

Celeste belonged to him, and he belonged to her.

Celeste stood at the entry and rapped her knuckles against the door jamb twice. "May I come in?" She had not hesitated to follow her grandfather into his study. The entire carriage ride home, he had been silent. Every time she tried to initiate a conversation, he merely grunted.

He blew out a breath and nodded. She considered that a good sign since he didn't roll his eyes.

"Come to find out about Grolier?" He pointed to a seat in front of his desk.

She walked across the gold and red Aubusson carpet with her confidence on full display and didn't look away as he scowled at her.

She settled into the proffered seat and clasped her hands in her lap. Without flinching, she studied the man who had so much influence over her future. Heavy wrinkles lined his eyes and brow. His jowls drooped like a hound that had seen too many hunting seasons. In the evening candlelight, he appeared to have aged years since the dinner at the Duke of Pelham's house.

Though anger seethed inside of her, she kept her voice calm. "I've never heard of the Marquess of Grolier. Is he even a real person?"

Her grandfather narrowed his eyes. "Remember I had luncheon with him not too long ago where we discussed you and marriage. He's about to enter his third decade. He owns the property directly to the east of Exehill Hall. I've always fancied the acreage. Besides expanding the largest sheep pasture, it will allow direct access to the canal that will shortly be built in the area. I plan on using it to haul coal to the city. It should be quite profitable for the dukedom."

"Well, I see what you're getting out of it, but help me see how that will benefit me."

Celeste had never spoken to her grandfather in such a direct manner. Perhaps it was knowing that Malcolm would support her in whatever she said, or perhaps, it was that she was finally seeing her grandfather in a new light. One that didn't mask his true intent in the matter. He didn't care about her or her happiness. He only wanted what a potential groom could give him.

For a moment, he stared at her with an open mouth. With a grim chuckle, he smiled her way. "Grolier will inherit his father's Scottish title. Their ducal estate is at the very tip of the northeast coast. It's colder there than anywhere else in Scotland. You'll have to dress in furs, I imagine."

She'd be sent to live in a remote part of Scotland away from her family and friends.

Away from Malcolm.

After a moment, her grandfather continued, "For the first time, I see a bit of your mother's spirit in you. When she decided to run away with *that man*, she told me I could do nothing to stop her. It was the first time she'd ever disobeyed me." He propped his elbows on his desk and leaned toward her. "It was the last time as well."

"What do you mean?"

"After that confrontation, your mother escaped to Gretna Greene and married that man. Upon word of the marriage and the fact that nothing could be done to annul it, I banished her from my sight. Then I sent my solicitor to their home with a short and brief letter apprising her. Imagine my surprise when I saw her at a soiree a month later. I gave her the cut direct."

They'd been estranged for over twenty-three years.

"You should have told me you were thinking of the match." Celeste didn't cower at his frown. "I should have met him to see if he and I would make a suitable match."

"There was no need. He'll be here tomorrow." Her grandfather flicked his hand as if chasing off an errant fly. "You said you'd marry whom I picked. You don't need to approve your bridegroom."

"It's my future," she said defiantly.

"It's my future as well," he spat, then narrowed his eyes. "Besides, don't you want me to welcome your mother back into my loving arms?"

"Based upon what you said at the Duke of Pelham's table about my parents, it appears that you've no intention of trying to heal the estrangement that exists between my mother and you." She tilted her chin. "You publicly displayed your full rancor toward my parents this evening."

He thrummed his fingers against the top of his desk and regarded her. "You've always wanted all of us to be one big happy family. But this evening, you seemed to lose interest. I wonder the cause. Perhaps you've set your sight on the Duke of Pelham." He rubbed his jaw. "I could approve such a match."

She studied her clasped hands. "I have no interest in the Duke of Pelham."

She'd been foolish and naïve to believe that by agreeing to submit to her grandfather's wishes, he would somehow forgive her mother. He'd called her a whore and her father a bastard just the other day. His grudge against her parents would never heal. She should have realized this months ago. It would have saved her so many hours of trying to please her grandfather. Whatever she had done to appease him in the past was never enough.

She was never enough.

"This has nothing to do with that man you sat next to at dinner this evening, does it?" He looked up to the ceiling. "Don't be foolish. I would never allow you to marry such a man. Millionaire or not. He's a man of trade. He works with his hands."

"And his mind," she argued. "Malcolm Hollandale is a gentleman. Any woman would be lucky to win his regard."

"Except for you," her grandfather murmured. "Need I remind you that your blood is blue? He's a commoner. He might as well be a blacksmith or candlemaker."

Celeste stood abruptly. "Why should you care about such things? Your first thought should be what would make me happy."

"Happiness doesn't guarantee success. You should know that by now. You're not a starry-eyed schoolgirl anymore. Your parents are a perfect example of an unsuccessful union. They're in debt to me. If your mother obeyed me, she'd be living in splendor instead of squalor.

"They have love," she said quietly. "That's a successful marriage."

"Frankly, I thought you were smarter than your mother. But if I'm not making myself clear, let me rephrase it. You will not marry beneath you. If you do, it'll cause a scandal. You don't want that. *You cannot want that. Therefore, you cannot marry Malcolm Hollandale*."

She stared at him and tilted her chin slightly. "I'm of age, and my parents would approve of him."

He *tsked* with a shake of his head. "Go ahead and do what you like. You'll discover on the morrow what your actions have caused."

Her heart thudded in her chest, warning her that she might have gone too far in her obstinance. "What do you mean?"

"One stroke of my pen, and I'll call in your father's note." He placed his hands on the desk then leaned forward, glowering at her with his gray eyes. "I can ruin Hollandale's reputation. He must be the father of your lady's maid's bastard. Why else would he hire a lady's maid, for God's sake? Anyone with half a brain would see that." He lifted a bushy white brow, challenging her.

Celeste blinked slowly as the horror of her situation floated around her. The man before her had no sense of familial love or obligations. He was only concerned with wealth and power.

She swallowed as she clenched her fists.

"He is not the father of Alice's baby. Alice told me who the father was." And under no circumstance would she tell her grandfather. At his skeptical scowl, she continued, "You would threaten to ruin a good, honest man to force me into a marriage that I don't want?"

"It's a good marriage. You should be grateful." He was eerily calm. "Have you seen your grandmother's prized teaspoons? They weren't in the silver closet this morning."

At the sight of his slight grin, a chill ran up her spine at his nonchalant tone. Did he know she'd taken them to Malcolm? Was he threatening her?

Of course he was.

He was also threatening Malcolm. The kind, sweet man who'd agreed to help Alice simply because Celeste had asked. Then he'd welcomed her into his home and showed her he was a man of honor and knew how to love. When he kissed her, he made her feel like she was the most important person in his world. She had little doubt he'd do anything to make her happy and would cherish her until the end of his days.

She loved him with every fiber of her being. She always had.

But love also meant that you protected each other. If she chose Malcolm over her grandfather, he'd be ruined. And she would be the one who caused it.

Tears burned her eyes and throat. She ached when she thought of the costs he'd have to pay to be with her. Her grandfather would destroy all his honor and everything he'd worked for over the years.

What a fool she'd been thinking she could have Malcolm and make him happy. That was never going to happen, but she could protect him. With her head held high, she turned to leave. No matter how bleak her future was, she'd protect her loved ones. She ignored her grandfather's chuckle as she closed the study door. Once outside, her heart splintered and fell into gossamer pieces of broken hopes and dreams.

Numb, Celeste went to her room, where Marianne, a newly hired lady's maid, waited for her inside. When the maid caught Celeste's gaze, she put a finger to her mouth, motioning her to be quiet. Celeste nodded and silently closed the door.

"Oh, ma'am, look at this precious bundle," Marianne whispered as she held out a woven basket where a little meow sounded.

Celeste hurried to the basket and gently lifted the lid. As soon as she did, a little white head of fur popped up, demanding attention. It was her kitten, her One. When the kitten saw her, she started to mewl loudly.

"Shush, little one," Celeste softly cooed as she lifted the kitten from its basket. She looked at Marianne and frowned slightly. "Where did she come from?"

Marianne instantly blushed and held out a piece of parchment. "I dunno." As soon as Celeste took the note, the maid stared at the ground. "I can't read, ma'am." Embarrassment tinted the maid's low voice.

As the kitten dug its claws into her bodice, Celeste held it with one hand, then reached out and placed her other hand on the girl's arm. "Thank you, Marianne." She dipped her head until her gaze met hers. "Plenty of people are employed at my grandfather's home who do not know how to read or write. But if you stay with me, I can help you."

The maid smiled hopefully as Celeste took the note.

"I'm lucky to have this position. I don't want to cause any trouble. Besides, I couldn't ask that of a fine lady like yourself."

"I would like to help," Celeste said softly. "I have all these books and no one to share them with." She waved a hand around the room where stacks of books were scattered haphazardly, but Celeste knew where every title was. She had even kept several grammar books from her youth. "I can teach you."

Marianne finally smiled. "I'd like that, ma'am."

Celeste nodded. "Good. Then it's decided." Without waiting another minute, she opened the note.

Dearest Duchess,

Neither One nor I could bear the thought that you would be alone without anyone to comfort you. Every kitten volunteered to keep you company, but One insisted she was the 'one' you liked best.

Every time you cuddle with her, imagine it's me. I'm sending all my affection with this little fluff of fur. I've also sent food and instructions on how to care for her.

I've told the kitten that it'll be a temporary stay as I fully intend to bring her and her mistress back to my home. We have much to discuss, my love, but needless to say, I want you in my life forever.

Send word if you need me, and I'll be there within ten minutes and shall whisk you away from your grandfather's machinations. You're mine, and I'm yours.

All my forevers,

M.

"Marianne, I'm going out." Gently, she put One back in her basket. There was no way she'd allow the kitten to stay here. Likely, the footman who answered the door knew exactly what was inside and told the butler that an animal was in the house. No doubt her grandfather would order her kitten thrown out or, worse, destroyed immediately.

"What shall I say if someone asks for you?" Marianne twisted her fingers and shifted her weight from foot to foot.

Celeste took one of her hands. "Look at me, Marianne." When the maid did as asked, Celeste continued in a low voice, "You are to go downstairs and say that you put me to bed with a megrim and intimate that I started my monthly courses. No one should bother me. If anyone asks about the basket, say you took it outside. Then go to bed. Now, come help me prop the pillows so it looks like I'm under the covers."

Within ten minutes, Celeste had snuck out the servants' entrance with the basket in tow. Malcolm's Mayfair home was three streets over. If she walked through the back-streets and alleys, no one would see her.

If she were forced to say goodbye, Celeste would do it her way.

She would do it in his bed.

CHAPTER ELEVEN

F resh from his bath, Malcolm took a sip of whisky and sat in front of the fire in his library. It was his favorite part of the day. He could relax in his banyan and not be disturbed. His servants had long since retired.

In the late evenings, Malcolm enjoyed the peace, quiet, and solitude of his Mayfair manse. It allowed him to contemplate his experiments, other work, and the upcoming days. He was always organized, but tonight, something else, or should he say, someone else stole his thoughts. His duchess.

If he had to do everything over again, he should have confronted Celeste's grandfather, then whisked her away with him. He'd have brought her here and convinced her to marry him. A common license would only require that they wait seven days. If need be, Celeste could stay at Pelham's house with his sisters or even Ravenscroft's home with his mother, Lady Ravenscroft.

He took another sip, then leaned his head against the sofa back and closed his eyes. God, he could almost smell her sweet rose fragrance. What he wouldn't give to have

Celeste curled against his side, making love in front of the fire, then holding each other's hands as they made their way upstairs. Whenever he'd daydreamed about a wife, he'd never pictured a face...until now. Now it was Celeste whom he imagined would share her life with him.

A soft meow broke his silence, and he opened his eyes. It was as if he'd conjured her from his dreams. There, in front of him, Celeste stood. He didn't speak. All he wanted to do was to drink in the sight of her.

She smiled and held the basket he'd sent over with both hands.

"Are you real?"

"Very much so."

When the kitten meowed again, Celeste carefully set down the basket and retrieved the white kitten. When she held it to her chest, the kitten latched onto her gown and crawled up her chest determined, it seemed, to crouch upon her shoulder.

"Darling, careful," she murmured as she tilted her head to give it more room. But her gaze never left his.

"How did you get in?"

She motioned to the floor-to-ceiling French doors off the terrace. "There. You don't lock them." She bit her lip. "I had to see you."

He exhaled a shuddered breath. Everything felt right in his world for the first time since he'd arrived home. Deliberately, he rose from the sofa and came toward her. Celeste's eyes skated down his chest to his feet and back up again.

Her eyes widened. "Are you retiring? Am I interrupting?"

"No." He continued to drink in her features as he stood before her. "I come down here in the evenings after I've bathed. It's peaceful." Carefully, he plucked the kitten from her shoulder and started to pet it. "You didn't like my gift?"

"I love your gift. She's precious, just like you." Tears welled in her eyes.

"I've never seen someone in love cry." He wiped away a tear. He smiled when she laughed.

Playfully, she swatted at him. "Who said I was in love?" A grin curved her lips as she reached over and stroked the kitten's fur.

When their fingers collided, Malcolm wove them together, then brought her hand to his lips. "A man can hope." The kitten was sound asleep, cradled in his other hand. He bent down and carefully laid the exhausted ball of fur on top of the soft bedding in the basket. "I'll take her to work with me on the morrow."

"I think it's for the best." Celeste wiped the remaining tears.

He cupped her cheek. "The kitten will always be yours."

"Thank you. I had no doubt my grandfather would dispose of her."

Malcolm growled at the injustice of it. Instantly, he pulled her into his arms and kissed her, pouring into it all his love and desire and his vow to protect her from any more ugliness. She had seen enough in her short life. Slowly, he pulled away, but he didn't let her go. "I wish I would have been there with you. I'd like to see what your grandfather would have said if I was there, and he'd discovered the cat."

Celeste ran her hands slowly up and down his chest, the soothing movement burning every inch of him. "I wouldn't want you to witness his viciousness." She tilted her gaze to his. "But I would have safeguarded you and our kitten with my life."

He lowered his forehead to hers. "My brave, beautiful protector. God knows how much I love you."

"I love you." She grabbed his lapels and stared into his eyes, signaling the significance of her declaration. "Always and forever. Promise me you'll remember that."

He nodded. It felt like a vow of marriage between them.

Slowly, he lowered his lips to hers, sealing their bond to one another. She wrapped her arms around his neck and softened against him. He deepened the kiss, and his beautiful duchess moaned her approval. This was always what he'd envisioned his life would be like with a wife who was as committed to him as he was to her. Unhurriedly, he swept his tongue against hers, the rhythm slow and deep, like a prelude before they made love.

"Is this a dream?" He trailed his fingers over her cheek, then pushed an errant lock of hair behind her ear.

Her blue eyes were more brilliant than sapphires. "No, but I need you." She spoke the words softly. "Tonight."

Malcolm stilled, searching her eyes for any hesitation or unease. Celeste's gaze never wavered.

Without waiting, he tossed pillow after pillow in front of the fireplace until it resembled a bed made for pleasure. He held her hand and touched it to his lips. "I must be honest. All I've thought about is making you mine."

Celeste's beautiful eyes were lit by the firelight, amber notes around her irises shining. The commitment between them was unmistakable.

The space between them disappeared as he wrapped her into his embrace. Her hands drifted into his hair as she anchored her mouth to his.

He lightly traced the rim of her lips with his tongue. He smiled when a slight moan escaped from Celeste. He moved his tongue against hers, mimicking what he'd do to her body. He ignored the voice in his mind, warning him to consider if this was a good idea. He didn't care. He wanted her.

He craved her. Celeste Worsley was as vital to him as the air that he breathed. He pressed her closer, his hardness meeting her softness, letting her know how much he desired her.

"Celeste," he moaned as he continued kissing her, devouring her, telling her with his caresses that she was his, and he was hers. She tasted of wine and berries and forever, a heady reminder that they were devoted to one another.

And he would never let her go.

"Help me undress," she sighed and turned around.

Unable to speak, he made quick work of the buttons on the back of her gown. As each one slipped free of its mooring, he pressed an opened-mouth kiss to her skin, then her stays. He felt as if he were drunk on her rose fragrance mixed with the scent of her arousal. For as long as he lived, he'd never forget it or this night.

The dress hung loosely about her body. She turned with a smile and pushed the gown from her hips, where it landed with a swoosh on the carpet. He held her hand as she stepped out of it, pushing it away with her foot. Never taking her eyes from his, she untied her stays and threw them. They landed on her dress. Quickly, she removed her shoes and stockings.

Malcolm's cock hardened at the sight. Only her chemise separated him from exploring every glorious inch of her.

She brought her hands to the simple chignon she wore, then unfastened the pins, one by one. When the dark silk of her hair fell about her shoulders, his breath caught.

Every strand glistened as if she and the entire night were enchanted.

"Open your banyan," she commanded.

He didn't have to be told twice. He loosened the fastenings, then quickly shed the silk garment.

Her eyes roamed over his body like an artist studying a model. Her breath hitched at the sight of his erect cock. "You're huge."

"You make me this way."

Her eyes slowly lifted from his cock to his chest. "You remind me of a painting I saw of Apollo. He looked just like you except"—she waved a hand down his body—"for down there. You're much bigger." Her gaze met his. "You're beautiful."

He bent his head to hide the heat that marched up his neck and bludgeoned his cheeks.

"Malcolm, did I say something wrong?" she asked softly.

He shook his head. "No one has spoken of me that way."

"It's the truth. You're the most handsome man I've ever seen. I fell in love with you the first time I saw you." Her voice softened. "May I touch you?"

He nodded, then took her hand. Never tearing his gaze from hers, he slowly wrapped it around his member. Her touch was so incredibly gentle and unbearable that he closed his eyes to savor it. He would come like an adolescent if she didn't unveil her body soon.

"Your skin reminds me of velvet, but it's hard beneath my fingers." She looked up at him as she stroked him. "And hot."

"Celeste, later, I will let you play with me to your heart's content, but it shall have to wait." He reached and pulled the tie on her chemise. "I want to see you. All of you."

She smiled again as she shimmied out of the muslin covering, and let it drop to the floor.

He simply stared for a moment, then sucked in a deep breath. Her breasts sat high on her chest, perfectly sized for him to hold in his large palms. His mouth watered as he thought of laving his tongue against her taut pinkish-brown nipples. His gaze slowly fell across her flat stomach and traced the width of her hips. He flexed his fingers. The need to hold her became nigh near unbearable.

But the brown nest of curls took his breath away. Her arousal glistened on her thighs. He licked his lips, ready to devour her. God, he'd never wanted a woman like he wanted Celeste.

"Say something," she murmured.

He grabbed his cock and fisted it at her innocent words. "Every time I've seen you, I thought you exquisite. But tonight, seeing you like this makes you even more so." He lowered his voice. "You're stunning. You steal my breath. Do you believe me?"

She nodded.

"Touch me," he urged. He pulled her hands to his chest. Instantly, she explored his body as he explored hers. Their kisses turned desperate at the deliciousness of finally being together after being far too long apart.

She trailed her fingers across his chest, down his stomach, until she touched his cock. The juxtaposition of her dainty fingers folded around his hard length elicited a primordial growl.

"Celeste." The whisper of her name sounded like a prayer upon his lips. He'd plead to the devil if she would continue caressing him.

A rainbow of colors from the fire flickered in the green

depths of her eyes. Her breath caressed his lips in a different type of kiss. He pulled her close until their bare chests were flushed against each other before he picked her up and gently laid her on the pillows.

"There might be pain the first time." He covered her body with his and rested his weight on his elbows. The firelight traced the map of freckles on her breasts, her stomach, and the sinuous lines along her thighs. He could spend a year studying her body and never grow tired of it. But he had to let her know that she was always safe with him. Always. This was her decision for them to share each other's bodies. "We don't have to do this tonight."

"I want everything with you." She rose up and wrapped her arms around him. Her fingers tightened in his hair. "Tonight, let me love you."

Celeste stroked the hair that had fallen across Malcolm's forehead. He shivered at the touch but never stopped staring at her. Softly, he growled his pleasure and pushed Celeste onto the pillow mattress beneath them.

He lowered his body against her chest and pressed his lips to hers. "I've wanted this night for so long. But I've wanted you for longer," he whispered in her ear.

"As have I," she answered.

Malcolm's warmth pressed against her, and he hissed slightly at the contact. His cock slid through her wetness. Every sensitive inch of her body quivered with anticipation. The feel of his naked body against hers invoked a pleasure she'd never tire of.

Her mind refused to stay quiet. She here with Malcolm, and nothing would stop them. She'd loved him from afar for years and might never get to be with him again. If she'd had any hesitation at all, it had flown across the sky like a kite in the wind.

It was gone, and she was glad for it.

He placed gentle kisses across her breasts and laved her achy nipples with his tongue. She closed her eyes and let the pleasure cascade through her. Gradually, he moved down her body and stretched her legs apart. She shivered as he tantalizingly dragged his tongue across her folds, then pulled them apart. His eyes darkened into a midnight blue, and a wicked smile curved his lips before his tongue lapped her sensitive nub. Her back arched in response to the pleasure rushing up her spine.

They had come so far since that fateful day in Drury Lane. She knew him better than she knew any other person. How fitting that she was sharing everything with him tonight. He was a master of pleasure, and she was losing herself with each stroke and touch he placed upon her body. Every sensation was heightened, and she desperately wanted to be lost in the pleasure of it all.

Malcolm spread her folds wider and swept two fingers gently back and forth across that tender spot. By then, she was panting. Her hands were fisted in the pillows as she arched her back, holding her climax at bay.

"Come for me," he commanded hotly. "Let me feel you squeeze my fingers. Imagine it's my cock inside of you, stroking and pleasuring you. You can't hold on any longer. Let me see you take your pleasure."

With his rough voice and wicked words, not to mention his thumb rubbing circles around her clitoris, she was on the precipice about to fall. Then the beautiful, dastardly man applied a perfect gentle pressure against the tender nub. The sensation was too much, and suddenly, she came undone entirely on his fingers. The pleasure was so great that she couldn't help but buck her hips. Waves of sensation rolled through her as he kept swirling her most sensitive skin.

Slowly, Celeste's body floated back under her control, but it still hummed with the orgasm he'd given her. Malcolm inched his way up her body, never tearing his gaze from hers. He licked his tongue along the seam of her lips. She wrapped her arms around him, and her mouth met his. She groaned at the taste of her arousal on his lips. It was wanton, but there was something tenderly sensual in the act. He'd pleasured her, all the while cherishing her. Malcolm drew her closer as his tongue delved deeper into her mouth.

A deep shudder ricocheted through her body. She moaned again as he held her. His muscles flexed as she wrapped her hand around his cock and guided it to her entrance.

She wanted to make love to him. But she could feel his restraint as she attempted to take him in another kiss. They were both panting as if they'd raced across the country-side. He levered his hand on the back of her head, keeping her in place so he could kiss her again.

"Celeste, are you…"

She put her hand on his lips. "Don't ask if I'm certain. Ask if I'm ready."

With a lop-sided smile, he asked, "Are you ready?"

His rough voice reminded her of a cat's tongue. At first, it was a bit jarring, but quickly, it was something to crave and cherish.

"I've waited for this my entire life. I am ready for the wait to be over."

He positioned his cock at her entrance. Never taking his gaze from hers, he inched inside of her. He tilted his hips slightly as he slid into her. She closed her eyes at the sudden fullness. He stopped for a moment, then pushed. She bit her lip at the sharp pinch.

Once fully seated, he murmured, "So bloody tight."

"Is that good?" She rubbed her hands up and down his back. The muscles instantly contracted. He was so powerful, yet he treated her like a rare piece of china.

"Very good. This is heaven," he murmured. Sweat beaded on his forehead, and the muscles on his arms bunched and trembled, revealing his restraint. He swept his lips against hers. "Put your legs around my hips.

She did as asked. Slowly, his hips moved against hers. The feeling of fullness continued, but there was no hint of pain left. Never tearing his gaze from hers, he withdrew little by little then pushed back in. She tightened her muscles, trying to keep him anchored to her. He closed his eyes as if in pleasure and gradually moved faster. He buried his head against her neck and crooned nonsensical words. *Cherish. Heaven. Mine.* In between uttering endearing terms, he pressed his lips to her neck, marking her and loving her simultaneously. She would never be the same after this and was glad for it. She would be his forever, and he would be hers.

Their skin slapped together every time he moved deeper in her. She held on to him as he buried his head against her neck. All she wanted was to be wrapped in his arms and pinned by him. Possessed by him.

"Malcolm," she cried as another release hit her with a force that stole her breath. She tightened around him, squeezing her eyes shut at the intensity that pulsed through her body.

By then, his hips were pounding against hers, moving like a piston as he chased his pleasure. He lifted his body and looked where they were joined. He tilted his head back, then grimaced as he shouted her name.

The rush of his hot release flooded her, and she wrapped her arms around him.

She'd found her sanctuary. Her place of peace. It was with him.

He buried his head against her shoulder, pressing tender kisses about her neck. He kept repeating her name like a litany. She smoothed her fingers through his hair and kissed his cheek over and over.

Eventually, his breathing slowed along with his heartbeat. After a few moments, he lifted himself and brushed his fingers across her forehead. Gently, he tipped her face so he could see her more readily.

His expression of profound love stole her breath. She kissed him and curled his blond locks around her finger. He returned her kiss with equal fervor and neediness, then rested his forehead against hers and shook his head slightly as if he didn't understand what had come over them. Something about the confusion in his eyes felt like a relief to her. It was as if the earth had exploded into a million pieces and had put itself together in the aftermath of their lovemaking.

They were sheltered in a perfect moment where the outside world couldn't find them, nor could it ruin what they'd shared. They were simply two people united in their love, the most precious gift they could share with one another.

But her sanctuary didn't last. Fear hung heavily around her like wolves ready to attack their prey. She feared that whatever passion she felt with Malcolm would come crashing down around her, and she would only be left with the havoc her grandfather had sown.

CHAPTER TWELVE

A gentle rain fell against the library's windows as Malcolm held Celeste. They were side by side, with her head resting on his shoulder. The gentle movement of her chest rose and fell, indicating she was dozing in his arms. He played with the tendrils of hair that adorned the side of her head. He'd covered her with his banyan to keep the chill away. The warmth of her body was a comfort he could look forward to from this day on.

When she woke, he'd formally ask her to marry him, and then they'd plan for him to visit her parents and ask the same. He smiled softly and pressed a kiss against her head as he thought of how their lives had changed so much in the last week and a half. They'd circled each other's orbits for so long, and now they would spend the rest of their lives together.

The longcase clock chimed twice. Celeste stirred in his arms.

"Rest," he murmured as he squeezed her gently.

She eased away from him and pushed her long dark tresses from her face as she stared at the clock. "It's so late. I must return home." She turned to face him. "Will you help me secure a hackney?"

"Absolutely not," he murmured, reaching over, and kissing her. "I'll take you home." He braced himself on one hand. His eyes searched hers. The pleasure in her gaze made her appear as if she were drunk from their lovemaking, and he felt the same. "Celeste, you're all I think about and everything I desire in life. You make me want to be a better person." He pressed a gentle kiss to her lips. "Will you do me the honor of agreeing to be my wife? You'll never want for anything, I promise."

She frowned slightly and took a deep breath. Everything inside him froze as his gaze searched her tear-filled eyes.

He knew at that moment that she would refuse him. "Tell me."

She placed her palm on his hand still cupped on her cheek, then stared at him. "I'm so honored that you asked me. But I can't."

"Because of this supposed betrothal with Grolier?" He sat up and cupped both of her cheeks. "Look at me, love." His thumbs rubbed the soft skin of her cheeks, and he vowed to catch every one of her tears and kiss them away. "I'll go see him and explain that we're in love with one another."

"Malcolm, that won't work." She stood slowly.

Her gracefulness reminded him of Venus rising from the ocean foam and standing on a pink shell that was the exact color of her beautiful lips.

She donned her chemise, then worked her stays. "My grandfather threatened that he'd foreclose on my parents' mortgage if I didn't do as he says. Damnation," she cursed as her fingers tangled in the cording.

"Let me help you." He stood naked before her, and her

eyes went to his semi-aroused cock. "That's what you do to me, always. Even if it was a short glimpse of heaven." He winked, gently batted her hands away, then started to attend to her. "I'll pay your parents' mortgage, so they're not beholden to him anymore." He pulled the strings tight and tied them in a neat bow, which was an appropriate description since he'd outlined a quick solution and resolution to her concerns about her parents. He pressed a kiss to her perfect nose.

"If only it were that easy," she murmured with a sad smile, then stepped into her gown. "But that's not all of it."

Malcolm helped straighten out the material that had bunched around her waist. She turned and presented him with her back. Just as he'd done before, whenever he fastened a button, he pressed a kiss to her exposed skin. Not an inch of her back, shoulders, and neck were ignored. When satisfied with his handiwork, he turned her to face him.

"What else?" He took her hands in his when he saw the stark fear that stole the gorgeous blush from her cheeks. She paled as if she'd seen a ghost. "Darling?"

"Grandfather said he'd ruin you." Her hands fluttered like butterflies having nowhere to alight.

"How?" he asked incredulously. "We don't have the same friends or acquaintances."

She shook her head and turned to stare out the window.

"Celeste?" He gently pulled her until she faced him again. "Whatever poison he spews, it won't hurt me."

She closed her eyes and tipped her head to the ceiling. "It's not that easy, Malcolm. He told me that if I don't do as he says, he'll tell everyone that you're the father of Alice's baby, and now, you've set her up as your mistress under the disguise of a maid. He's always been ridiculously melodramatic and obsessed with morality."

"Your parents' banishment is a perfect example," he said gently.

She fisted both hands as a blush covered her cheeks. "I will not allow him to hurt Alice. And I will *never* allow him to hurt you with those lies. You're the kindest and most generous man I know. He'll decimate you and your goodness with his evil by spreading these falsehoods."

At the vehemence in her words, his heart skipped a beat. Her righteousness and passion were glorious. If he'd thought her beautiful before, he'd been mistaken. She was *magnificent*, a warrior who would protect him at all costs. He vowed to protect her with the same fervor.

He wiped away the solitary tear that trickled down her cheek, then took her hands in his. "Listen to me, love. He doesn't have the power to hurt me."

She shook her head. "You don't know him the way I do."

"Let me take care of your parents, and I'll worry about the rest later. Your grandfather's lies will not have the power to wound me. Alice and Benjamin are married. That proves that your grandfather's bluster is for naught."

She swallowed. "You'd do that for my parents?" Immediately, she shook her head. "I can't ask that of you."

"You're not asking it of me. I'm doing it because I want to help your parents. And I'll do it for you. I don't want you to worry. We'll find a way out of your grandfather's macabre web to keep us apart.

"Thank you." She nodded, a tremulous smile on her lips. "I trust you. Together, we'll find a solution to this scheme my grandfather has placed in our laps."

"I do like the sound of together." He waggled his eyebrows. His heartbeat accelerated at the grin on her face. "May I call on you tomorrow?" He lifted his brow. "We can discuss our marriage plans."

She shook her head, then picked up her kitten, who'd climbed out of the basket after her nap. She pressed a kiss to the top of the kitten's head. "Let me send you a note, and we'll meet somewhere. My grandfather will become suspicious if you call on me at his home. He won't think anything of my shopping." She placed the kitten back in its basket, where it curled up again.

Malcolm eyed the white kitten. He had never been jealous of one of his cats, but One was attempting to steal her mistress's heart.

"You have all my firsts. You were the first and only man I fell in love with. The first man I truly kissed. The first man I made love to."

"And the only man you'll make love to." He clasped her shoulders and rubbed his thumbs slowly against her silken skin.

Celeste smiled in his direction. "Take care of One until I return. Perhaps you should dress if you plan to take me home."

"That's not your home anymore. Your home is here... with me." Malcolm kissed his duchess, his future wife. He turned and left the room to dress. No way in hell would her grandfather keep Malcolm away from Celeste.

She was his, forever.

And one thing he knew from studying chemistry. Some bonds are never meant to be broken.

Just like the one he and his duchess shared.

The next morning, Celeste checked her appearance in the cheval mirror that stood sentry in her bedroom. She'd returned to her grandfather's home safely last night.

Malcolm had gallantly walked her to the servant's door. He wouldn't leave until she had waved at him from her bedroom window. Thankfully, the entire house was quiet, as no one was in the kitchen. The butler and housekeeper were abed. The footmen, standing guard at the front door, hadn't heard her enter.

She'd made her way up the servants' stairs without a single creak. When she'd left last night, she'd placed an inconspicuous piece of paper where the door met the door jamb to see if anyone had entered her room while she was gone. Thankfully, it was still in the same place.

When she'd waved goodbye to Malcolm, her heart had overflowed. He loved her and would ensure she and her parents were safe from her grandfather's designs to manipulate her into doing what he wanted. As she watched Malcolm walk down the alleyway to his awaiting carriage, she felt like she'd left her whole heart with him. A weight had been lifted off her shoulder by the time she'd left Malcolm's home last night.

She smiled. *Their home.*

She had complete faith in him and complete faith in them together. They would find a way to rectify the situation and marry.

She stood before the mirror to see if there was any indication that she'd changed since last night. Though she looked the same, she wasn't the same woman who'd ventured out in the dark of night to save a kitten and the man she loved more than anyone else in the world. She had no regrets about giving herself to Malcolm. The tenderness and care he'd shown her last night made her feel cherished, but the passion they'd shared would be engraved upon her heart forever. She'd never dreamed of finding a love that filled her entire being with happiness and security.

No matter what happened in her future, Celeste knew she'd love him forever.

And she suspected he felt the same as her.

A knock sounded, and Marianne entered her room. "Miss, His Grace is waiting for you in his study. He sent Mrs. Portland to tell me to fetch you."

"Thank you, Marianne." Celeste glanced at the Ormolu clock on her dressing table. She'd slept late, but she'd awoken in time for luncheon. She was none the worse for wear for her late night. If anything, she possessed a look of happiness, not to mention a hint of determination. Now, all she had to do was be a dutiful granddaughter until she left and met Malcolm.

With a confident step, she made her way downstairs. The door to her grandfather's study was open, and she entered with her head held high.

As soon as her grandfather saw her, he smiled. "Come in, dear. Come in. I have someone I want you to meet."

Celeste smiled, but the hair on her arms stood at attention. Something was off. She turned to greet the stranger who stood upon her arrival. He was a handsome man, a bit older...perhaps thirty or so. He commanded attention with an open smile, hair blacker than the night, and startling gray eyes. As he walked toward her, it was easy to tell he was fit and did not over-imbibe in heavy food or drink.

"Miss Worsley, it's a pleasure to meet you. I'm Caleb Starling, the Marquess of Grolier. Your grandfather has told me so much about you." He extended his hand to hers.

For a moment, she grappled for anything to say.

"Celeste," her grandfather hissed

The curt reprimand of her name on her grandfather's lips broke her from her musings. Immediately, she curtseyed, then extended her hand to his. "The pleasure is all mine, my lord."

Lord Grolier took her hand and gracefully bowed over it, then smiled.

She supposed it was a pleasant greeting, but it didn't make her toes curl in pleasure. Only Malcolm's smile could do that.

Then all her forgotten etiquette lessons came to her rescue. "Did you have a pleasant trip? I've heard the roads can be treacherous coming through the Highlands." She clasped her hands in front of her.

"Indeed, I did. However, I've been in London on business for my father for the last several weeks." He tilted his head and studied her. "I believe I might have seen you at Drury Lane once."

"I am quite fond of the theatre." Heavens, but she sounded like a ninny. She'd never been this out of sorts before in her life. But if her grandfather had his way, she'd be married to the man standing before her. Her heart pounded against her ribs at such a thought. She willed herself to calm down. Her future was with the man she loved, and she would not allow her dreams of a life with Malcolm to slip through her grasp.

"Come sit down," her grandfather instructed. "Grolier and I were discussing the arrangements." He pointed to the sitting area where the marquess had been sitting. "We were just about finished. I wanted you to join us for luncheon."

"Lovely," she murmured. "What arrangements?"

Her grandfather glowered at her. "Marriage arrangements."

Celeste stumbled at the words. "Pardon me?"

Grolier still wore the same smile, but lines creased his brow.

Don't be obtuse, girl," her grandfather murmured.

Slowly, Celeste approached the green velvet sofa but never took her eyes off the marquess. Once she was seated, both men followed. The marquess sat on the matching sofa across from her. When he smiled this time, sympathy shined in his eyes.

She straightened her spine. There was a tea service on the table. "Would you like for me to pour?"

Her grandfather nodded.

As she reached for the pot of hot water, her hands shook, betraying her unease.

The marquess frowned. "If we're to have luncheon, perhaps tea isn't necessary."

Celeste smiled in gratitude and placed her hands in her lap.

Her grandfather nodded but kept his attention on the marquess. "Celeste shall need to rest this afternoon to look presentable at the soiree tonight."

"Soiree?" Her gaze turned to her grandfather.

"Lord and Lady Cathcurt's soiree," her grandfather said dismissively.

Celeste tried to swallow her unease, but it was stuck in her throat like an unwanted frog. There had been no discussion of going out this evening. It was unlike her grandfather to attend social events on consecutive nights.

The butler, Thomason, entered the room. "Your Grace, Lord Grolier's room is prepared."

"Excellent," her grandfather drawled as he and the marquess stood. "Thomason, will you escort his lordship upstairs?"

The butler bowed.

Lord Grolier came to Celeste's side and took her hand. "Until later, Miss Worsley."

Celeste feigned a smile and nodded her head.

As soon as the butler and the marquess left the room, her grandfather turned to her. "I expect you to be ready for that soiree before Grolier thinks you're hesitant to marry him."

She held her stomach with her hand, preparing to do battle with her grandfather. "Why are you being so secretive? You're afraid that I won't agree to this." She didn't add that he was wise to have such suspicions.

"I know where you were last night. You ran to your precious Mr. Hollandale!" He laughed with a sneer. "You're just like your mother. You have the morals of an alley cat. After I announced your betrothal at Pelham's house, you've done nothing but fight me every step of the way. I'm trying to make this easier for both of us. It's the match of the Season." Her grandfather stalked to the library table and picked up a piece of parchment. "Do you know what this document is? Your marriage settlement. Both Grolier and I signed it this morning." He waved it in the air at her. "This is a binding contract."

"But I'm of age. Don't I have to sign it as well?" she challenged.

His mouth tilted in a half smile. "Do you think you'll find a solicitor who will agree to represent you in a dispute against me? My darling girl, don't forget who has the power here. I'm a respected member of the aristocracy. A duke no less." He puffed up his chest. "You're the daughter of a poor viscount who can't even afford to present you to society. Your parents gladly shipped you here. Practically begged me," he spat.

With an effort akin to fighting a bog that threatened to swallow her, Celeste stood though her legs threatened to collapse beneath her. How could she not have predicted this outcome? As the Seasons passed, he had become more unpleasant than the last.

"If that's all, *Your Grace*?" she murmured.

Her grandfather nodded. "Don't disappoint me. You

won't like the results. By and by, neither will your Mr. Hollandale."

Celeste paused for only a moment, then turned on the ball of her foot. As gracefully as her nerves would allow, she left the room. Once again, her grandfather threatened to ruin her loved ones. She had little doubt that her darling Malcolm would protect her parents. Who would protect him from a bitter old man?

A chill skated down her spine once she was outside the library door. This was exactly how a fly must feel when caught in a spider's web. No matter how much one fought against being captive, the deeper one became mired.

But she wouldn't quit fighting, even if the spider bit her.

There were two things to do. Firstly, she had to write Malcolm a note instructing him not to attend the soiree tonight.

Secondly, she would save Malcolm herself.

CHAPTER THIRTEEN

Malcolm hadn't stepped foot in his laboratory all day. He'd spent the day pacing after he received a note from Celeste asking him not to attend the Cathcurt soiree that evening. He studied the letter again to divine why she wouldn't want him there.

Initially, he planned to join the party as several men from Pelham's Millionaires Club with investment expertise were attending this evening. Malcolm had received a small fortune from one of the new glazes he'd created. He planned on placing half of the profit in an account at Lady Emma Somerton's bank, E. Cavensham Commerce, a bank for women run by women, for Celeste's private use. She could do anything with the monies. The other half, he would place in an investment portfolio he was creating for her. Every year, he'd put the investment profits into her banking account. He never wanted her or her family to be beholden to her grandfather's puppeteer ways ever again.

But now, his primary reason for attending was to see how she fared after their night together. He'd be lying if he didn't admit that he'd thought about her every hour last night. He could still smell her fragrance on his skin after he'd bathed. Immediately, he smiled. She was his happiness and future, and he was determined to give her those things as well. That meant that her grandfather would never threaten her again.

"Thank God, you're here," Pelham entered his study like the north wind, ready to conquer all in its path. "You need me."

"To what do I owe for this unexpected pleasure?" Malcolm smiled. Even if the duke could infuriate a sweet milk cow with his wily ways, he had a good heart.

"I'll think of payment when it suits me," the duke drawled as he threw his greatcoat on a side chair along with his walking stick and tall beaver hat. He pulled at his waistcoat as if preparing for a meeting with his solicitors, then regarded Malcolm from head to foot and lifted a brow. "You slept with her. Didn't you?"

Malcolm narrowed his eyes and lowered his voice until it resembled the growl of a lone wolf. "Have a care about whom you speak of, *Your Grace*."

Pelham rolled his eyes and raised his hand in a motion for Malcolm to stop. "Please. No drama. We have enough to worry about without that." He lifted a perfect aristocratic brow. "Whisky?"

Malcolm turned on his heel and strolled to the drum table, where he had an assortment of beverages for whenever his friends visited.

He poured two fingerfuls of the smokey liquor into cut crystal glasses, then handed the duke one. By then, Pelham sat before Malcolm's massive, burled wood desk.

He leaned one hip against the front of the desk and regarded the duke. They lifted their glasses, saluted each other, then gulped down the vital spirits.

The duke coughed and set down his empty glass. "That

will certainly clear any proverbial London fog clouding the brain. Now, as I was saying, Celeste Worsley came to see me—"

"What?" Malcolm asked incredulously as he sat down his empty glass. He crossed his arms and rested his backside against the desk to face the duke. "Why would she visit you?"

"I'll explain." The duke took a deep breath and then exhaled. "She's an exceptionally brilliant woman."

"I know," he said brusquely.

Pelham nodded. "Naturally, you'd be attracted to her. If I'd known her better, I would have given you a run for your money."

When Malcolm growled his disapproval, Pelham raised his hand in surrender. "She's yours. She made that clear when she was sitting in my study. Seems her grandfather had Lord Grolier in his pocket all along. Celeste explained that when she came down for luncheon today, her grandfather introduced her to Grolier and showed her the signed marriage settlements. After Grolier left to get settled in his rooms, her grandfather threatened that if she didn't marry the marquess, he'd ruin you and her parents without any reservation."

"I'll kill the man if he forces her to marry the marquess." Malcolm stood and motioned for the duke. "I'm leaving to finish this now. She'll not be under Exehill's thumb any longer. I promise you that."

"Spare me from men in love." Pelham shifted his gaze to the ceiling, then shook his head, upsetting his too-long blond hair. "So primeval. Now, sit down."

"You'd feel the same way if you were about to lose the woman you gave your heart to." Malcolm didn't shy away from sharing his emotions with the duke. There was nothing he wouldn't do to protect Celeste from harm.

"I know you and she discussed this last night," Pelham said. "But after what happened today, she's worried about you and your reputation. She's trying to protect you."

"But why didn't she come to me?" Malcolm glanced at One. The tiny white kitten tumbled into the room and made a beeline for Pelham. When the kitten noticed the shiny black boot on his long leg, she crept forward, ready to attack with her little tail twitching.

Completely oblivious that he was about to be ambushed, Pelham nodded. "It's an excellent question. It's why I came straight here after she left. She had a suspicion that the old duke was having her followed. Apparently, he referred to where she was last night." Pelham lifted an eyebrow. "I wonder where that was?" He lowered his voice, not hiding his sarcasm.

When Malcolm opened his mouth to send the duke a biting retort, Pelham lifted an aggravating eyebrow.

One decided that it was the perfect moment to attack. She crouched low, then leaped, throwing her entire body airborne toward the duke.

And completely missed him.

"What do we have here?" Pelham scooped the kitten into his large palm and brought her to his lap. As he moved his hand to pet her, One latched her paws around his hand, then started to kick her back legs with every bit of strength she could muster.

The average person would have thrown the kitten to the ground. Though her claws were little, they could still draw blood. But Pelham grinned at the kitten and brought her to his face. "You are fearless, my puss. But you'd best behave, or I'll sic my favorite retriever on you."

The kitten's eyes widened, and she went utterly still.

"That's better," Pelham said to the kitten as he brought her to his chest, where she instantly calmed and began to purr. He continued as if nothing untoward had happened. "Celeste came to me under the pretense that she was visiting Honoria and Pippa. But really, she wanted me to give you a message. Your woman is quite clever."

"She is mine." The words were out before Malcolm could withdraw them. Yet, he nodded at the admiration in the duke's voice. "She is *very* clever."

The unbridled urge to storm into the Duke of Exehill's home took root. His lip twitched into a sneer. But he forced himself to take a calming breath. It wouldn't do Celeste any good if he arrived at her grandfather's home half-cocked. He needed a plan. "What else did she say?"

"The old duke wants to formally announce the betrothal this evening at the Cathcurt soiree. You and I will be there with your solicitor to stop him from making a grave mistake that will ruin his reputation. Your Celeste came up with the plan." Pelham waggled his eyebrows. "She believes that the marriage agreement is null and void. I think she's correct. Celeste is of legal age. Therefore, she can say yes or no to the marriage. The old duke may be bargaining for property in exchange for Celeste's hand, but he's forgetting something. Celeste. What does she get out of the settlement?"

"Nothing now," Malcolm murmured.

"Exactly," Pelham exclaimed as if Malcolm was his star pupil. "Her grandfather threatened her parents, but you've generously volunteered to pay off their mortgage."

Malcolm nodded. "My solicitor is on his way to Exehill's solicitor's office. I've instructed him to pay it in full."

"Then that only leaves your reputation that we must concern ourselves with." Pelham grinned slyly. "Celeste and I have planned for all of your friends to be there and to spread the word about how you saved her lady's maid from being humiliated and thrown out on the street when it was discovered she was carrying." He leaned close as if divulging a secret. "That's what happened to Celeste's mother. Her father humiliated her in front of the servants. That's why she eloped. Within a matter of hours, the tale will be spread throughout London. Any negative words the old duke throws out about you will backfire. He'll be the one whose reputation will suffer."

The vise around Malcolm's chest loosened for the first time since Pelham entered his study. "So, she's not marrying Grolier?"

"Good God, no," Pelham said in horror. "Didn't you hear a word that I was saying? What would make you think that?"

That empty feeling of never being enough rolled around his chest. He was a grown man, but the taunts he'd suffered at Eton continued to haunt him. "I...I always thought perhaps it was too good to be true." Malcolm's shoulders fell. "Even though you, Ravenscroft, and Trafford treat me as equals, the truth is I'm a commoner and will always be one. My fellow students at Eton reminded me of that often enough once they found out about my being on scholarship. Celeste would be a duchess someday if she married the man."

Pelham put the kitten on the soft rug, then stood. "I could see how that would be a concern for you." He lowered his voice and put an arm around Malcolm's shoulder. "A man shouldn't be judged on the circumstances of his birth, no matter who he is. He should only be judged on how he behaves and what he values. We all should be held to that standard. Trust me when I say that there is no finer man than you. It's a privilege to call you my friend."

Malcolm's throat tightened at the sincerity of the

duke's words. "Thank you. I don't know what I did to deserve your friendship."

Pelham tapped his cheek with his finger, as if thinking. "Well, remember when you told me that I needed to invest with you after you made that new glaze for English bone china? I earned three thousand pounds the next year from that endeavor. That was the event that secured our friendship for me. Was it the same for you?"

Malcolm rolled his eyes and didn't answer.

Pelham laughed. "I believe you've forgotten something."

Malcolm tilted his head.

The duke lowered his voice. "Celeste Worsley will still be a duchess if she marries you. You've been calling her that moniker since you met her." Pelham smiled, then grew serious. "She loves you. Savor that and keep it precious."

"I promise." He rang a bell to call for his carriage. He would always safeguard her heart. "But Celeste's plan will have one deviation."

"What's that?" the duke asked.

"I'll be at the soiree front and center. I want a front-row seat to the entire affair."

"Excellent." Pelham smiled, petted the kitten, then turned suddenly serious. "Speaking of paying me, may I have a kitten?"

With Marianne accompanying her, Celeste had borrowed Amelia's carriage again. Her friend was generous beyond words. If Celeste had taken out one of her grandfather's carriages, the news of her meeting with Alice would have arrived at her grandfather's home before she'd exited the carriage.

"Miss, there's Alice," Marianne said softly as she pointed out the carriage window.

Instantly, Celeste knocked on the roof, a signal that they were to stop there. The coach pulled over in seconds, and a footman opened the door. Celeste was the first to exit, followed by her new lady's maid.

Alice didn't acknowledge her when she glanced her way. Instead, Celeste's friend turned on her heel and entered The Hungry Mind bookstore. It had become their meeting place since Alice had moved out of Exehill House.

"Ma'am, we'll pull the coach over there." The footman pointed toward the next block.

"Thank you. When we're finished, we shall find you." Celeste turned to her maid. "Come, Marianne."

Her maid followed, and soon they entered the store.

"Morning, Miss Worsley." The shopkeeper, Mr. St. Aulyn, nodded. "We have several new books of Wordsworth's in this week."

Celeste smiled. "You knew exactly where I was headed, did you not, sir?"

Mr. St. Aulyn smiled broadly. "Indeed. I always aim to keep my best customers in an abundant supply of books and happy."

"And you do a marvelous job of it, sir." Celeste continued forward.

As soon as they were hidden from view, Alice rushed forward and took Celeste's hands. "I came as soon as I received your note, Miss."

"As you are a married lady, you should call me Celeste." She squeezed Alice's hands and fought the burn of threatening tears. "You're my friend."

"I shall remember that." Alice's smile faded a bit. "But tell me your news." She glanced at Marianne and nodded.

The lady's maid turned toward the shop door to watch, ensuring no one interrupted them.

Celeste released a deep breath. "My grandfather announced at the Duke of Pelham's dinner party that I'm to marry the Marquess of Grolier." When Alice furrowed her brow, she continued. "I don't even know the man."

"What about Mr. Hollandale," Alice said softly. "You're in love with him, aren't you?"

Bemused, she shook her head. "I'm that transparent?"

"Well, when he walks into the room, and your face brightens like a firework display over Vaux Hall, it's an easy tell." Alice smiled affectionately and leaned near. "It's exactly the way I feel about Benjamin."

"It's uncanny. For once, I feel as if everything I've ever wanted was about to come true until my grandfather—" She cleared her throat and straightened her shoulders. There was no time to cry. She needed to get word to Malcolm about what had occurred. "I believe my grandfather suspects what my true feelings are for Malcolm. That's why he's doing the inconceivable."

"What?" Alice asked. The worry in her voice was evident.

"He told me that if I don't accept Lord Grolier, he'll ruin Malcolm by saying he's..." How to say the rest of it without hurting her friend?

"He's what, Celeste?" Nervously, Alice shifted her feet.

If Celeste wanted to protect Alice and her beloved Malcolm, then the only way to do that was to tell her everything. "Grandfather will say that Malcolm is the father of your baby. That's why he hired you." When Alice opened her mouth, Celeste pulled her near and lowered her voice. "It's a way to ruin him in front of everyone. Grand-father wants Malcolm to stay away from me."

"As if that's going to happen," Alice huffed. "My Benjamin won't like this at all."

Celeste smiled slightly at the vehemence in Alice's voice. "Neither will Malcolm. But that's not all. Grandfa-ther had planned to accuse you of stealing my grandmoth-er's prized silver teaspoons. He had planned to have you transported for stealing."

"What?" Alice's eyes went wide with fear.

"Please do not worry. I knew where the teaspoons were, so I took them myself. Malcolm has them." Celeste put her arm around Alice. "I wouldn't allow Grandfather to hurt you with those lies. But tonight, I fear Grandfather will humiliate Malcolm in front of the guests at Lord and Lady Cathcurt's soiree."

Alice rested her forehead in the palm of her hand. "What shall we do?"

Celeste placed her hands on Alice's shoulder. "Listen to me. Everything will be all right. I went to see the Duke of Pelham to tell him what was afoot. He'll help me protect Malcolm, but I'm worried for you. I've asked Amelia if you could stay at her home until this ends. Grandfather will believe that you're still at Malcolm's workshop." The tinkling of the bell above the door heralded the arrival of another customer. "Tell Benjamin what I've told you, then go to Amelia's immediately. I'll send word when it's safe to return to Benjamin. If need be, I can send you to my parents' home. They'll protect you."

Alice nodded as she squeezed Celeste's hand. "Thank you."

"Do not thank me yet." Celeste brought her into a hug. "I'll send word through Amelia. If you need to contact me, Amelia knows how to find me."

Alice squeezed her tight. "I don't know what to say." Embarrassed, she pulled away. "To say I'm sorry isn't enough. If I hadn't gotten myself into such a mess, you wouldn't have to—"

"Hush," Celeste said with a smile. "My grandfather would have found another way to keep me from Malcolm."

"Good luck with Mr. Hollandale." Alice smiled. "He adores you as well."

"We'll see what happens this evening. With the Duke of Pelham standing by his side, my grandfather's accusations won't hold. Hopefully, Lord Grolier sees what type of man my grandfather is and decides he has had enough." Celeste looked at the door again. "I must go. Wait five minutes and then go to the counter before you leave. Mr. St. Aulyn has several books for you. They're on my account."

Without another word, Celeste turned and then collected Marianne. She'd done everything she could to prepare for tonight's soiree. Hopefully, it wouldn't be anywhere near dramatic as a Drury Lane production.

CHAPTER FOURTEEN

The only sound in the carriage was the muted click-clack of the horses' hooves pounding the road as Celeste, her grandfather, and Lord Grolier made their way to Lord and Lady Cathcurt's soiree. It promised to be quite the crush, as everyone in society appeared to have been invited.

Celeste said a small prayer hoping that tonight would turn out as she'd hoped. Alice would be safe. Celeste would not be betrothed to the Marquess of Grolier.

And most importantly, Malcolm's reputation would be intact without even a volley being thrown by her grandfather.

"Whoa," the coach driver called out as they approached the Cathcurt's manse. They were still two blocks from where footmen waited to unload guests and direct the carriage traffic. Even from there, the calls and shouts of "move along" and "next" drifted into the carriage.

"Are you looking forward to tonight, Miss Worsley?" the marquess asked quietly.

Before she could answer, the duke turned their way. "Call her Celeste. You'll be marrying the girl tomorrow."

"Tomorrow?" Celeste's gaze shot to the marquess, who had the good sense to blush in embarrassment.

"Your Grace, Miss Worsley and I haven't had a chance to become acquainted yet." The marquess sat on the bench opposite her and her grandfather. His long legs were folded awkwardly, much like the uncomfortable lack of conversation in their coach. He glanced her way and smiled in reassurance. "I don't think it would be in either of our interests to rush into such matters until we are at ease with one another."

"You're not changing your mind, are you?" her grandfather asked. The hint of boredom in his voice was deceptive, but she'd heard it before. He always sounded that way before he'd strike like a viper, not caring who was in his way when he was spewing his poison.

"About marrying your granddaughter? No," the marquess answered in a tone that held a hint of rebuff. "There was never any mention when the marriage would take place." The marquess lifted a single brow. Directed at her grandfather, his daunting expression glowed in the lamplight.

Celeste glanced out the window again to see if she could see the Duke of Pelham's carriage in the line. He was crucial to tonight's success.

They'd inched their way to the head of the line. One of the Exehill footmen opened the door of the coach. The marquess was the first to exit. He held out his hand for Celeste to take. When she placed her hand in his, he squeezed gently and leaned near. "A yes or no will suffice. You didn't know anything about me, did you?"

By then, her grandfather had exited the carriage.

"Welcome, Your Grace," the Cathcurt's under-butler

called out. "May I have someone assist you to the entrance?"

Her grandfather scowled. "I walk just fine." He looked around the curved drive. "We should have arrived later. There are too many people to contend with."

As her grandfather nattered on, Celeste caught the marquess's gaze. "No," she whispered.

He pursed his lips at her answer, then nodded.

"Grolier, escort Celeste inside. I'll follow. It'll make a good appearance for all of us." Her grandfather pointed in the direction of the front entrance.

The marquess nodded and extended his arm. She could feel the tension in his muscles when she wrapped hers around his. He appeared livid at her grandfather's behavior.

"Ah, there you are, Exehill," the Duke of Pelham announced as he stepped beside her grandfather.

Celeste's breath caught. Malcolm came out of the shadows and stood by Pelham's side.

Lords Trafford and Ravenscroft stood beside Malcolm, along with Benjamin and another man she didn't recognize. By the looks on all their faces, their meeting was not by happenstance, nor did it appear to be a jovial greeting between friends.

Her gaze flew to Malcolm's, and his eyes locked with hers. His look could only be described as fierce. His perfectly fitted evening attire framed his body, emphasizing his strength. The set of his jaw declared he was a man not to be denied.

And not to be denied her.

As Pelham engaged her grandfather, Malcolm came forward. "Miss Worsley, my evening promises to be memorable with you here." He took her gloved hand and brought it to his mouth as he bowed.

Lord Grolier's eyes narrowed at the intimate contact.

When Malcolm rose, he didn't let go of her hand as he nodded to Grolier. His stare was steady and direct, claiming her as his. A smattering of goosebumps flew across her arms at his intensity. She'd be lying if she didn't admit his possessiveness thrilled her.

"Introduce me, please," his gravelly voice was low.

She squeezed Malcolm's hand. "Of course." She turned to the marquess. "Lord Grolier, may I introduce you to Mr. Malcolm Hollandale?"

"I'd be honored," the marquess said politely and extended his hand. "I'm Caleb Starling, the Marquess of Grolier."

Malcolm examined the man's hand. He appeared to be judging whether the marquess was worthy of his time. Only after a long moment that seemed to stretch into the next century did he release her and shake the marquess's hand.

"Are you a friend of Miss Worsley?" the marquess asked.

Malcolm leaned in and lowered his voice so no one else could overhear him. "To call me a friend deeply understates our feelings for one another."

Lord Grolier's eyes widened, and he took a step back. His gaze flew to Celeste.

She nodded.

But before she could say a word affirming their affection for one another, her grandfather grabbed her elbow. "What's all this?"

Slowly, Malcolm turned in the direction of her grandfather. One lip tugged in a sneer as Malcolm's gaze slowly fell to where the duke clutched Celeste's arm.

"Unhand her," Malcolm growled.

Her grandfather normally didn't abide by anyone

issuing ultimatums, but there must have been something in Malcolm's predatory stare that shocked him. Her grandfather quickly released her but didn't move from her side.

"Grolier," her grandfather said smoothly. "Mr. Hollandale fancies himself besotted with my granddaughter. He's a simple man of trade who relishes making a nuisance of himself everywhere." He raised his voice, ensuring others heard him. "Once you marry Celeste, I would advise you to take heed. Hollandale is not someone you want to associate with. He's impregnated one of my servants and then moved her into his shop where they live in sin."

The chattering of the servants and other guests who'd just arrived fell silent. Even the creak of approaching carriages stopped as the first attack against Malcolm was lobbed.

Celeste sucked in a breath as her heart slowly cracked in two. Everything she'd tried to prevent from happening tonight was unfolding before her eyes. She placed her hand on Malcolm's arm to comfort him and selfishly, to comfort herself with his strength.

"It's not true," she announced. She turned to Grolier to deny her grandfather's words when Ravenscroft once again came forward and stood on one side of Malcolm. Lord Trafford came to his other side. They stood tall and wide, an invincible wall. If her grandfather attacked Malcolm, then he would attack the other men.

A crowd, hungry for more of the melodrama to unfold, had gathered around the group.

The Duke of Pelham turned and faced her grandfather. "I wish you hadn't done that," he said disdainfully. "As your peer, I abhor becoming involved in other dukes' bad behavior and pettiness." Pelham tsked as he shook his head. "But you appear to relish digging the hole you're about to fall into."

Her grandfather narrowed his gaze.

Benjamin came to stand beside Malcolm. "I'm married to the maid you referred to. I'm the father of her unborn child. Mr. Hollandale was generous when he allowed her to come live with me and paid for the common license." He pointed to her grandfather. "The duke withheld her last month's wages for pure spite after she left his employment."

The crowd gasped collectively. Thankfully, such treatment of loyal servants was frowned upon by the majority of people in the *ton*. It was rare for a servant to publicly comment on a peer's bad behavior. No matter how true.

Pelham squinted his eyes as if in pain. "Exehill, you didn't?"

"He did," Malcolm added as his nostrils flared, betraying his anger. "After the servant had been with Miss Worsley for over eight years. He didn't even consult his granddaughter about firing the servant. He even made threats of bringing criminal charges against her, a loyal, loving employee who was treated abominably." His gaze toward her grandfather was sharper than a dagger. "You're simply trying to ruin my reputation because I love your granddaughter."

Now, the crowd gasped even louder.

Someone called out, "Why go to Drury Lane? Real life is so superior to any performance on the stage."

When the crowd chuckled, her grandfather fisted his hands. "It makes little difference. Celeste is marrying Grolier." He tilted his chin. "I'm announcing it this evening."

Pelham glanced at the crowd, then turned to the duke. "Shall we take this inside to someplace more private? No need to invite all of London to hear the scandal."

"I don't want to go anywhere," her grandfather snapped.

"You should have listened to Pelham, *Your Grace*." The derogatory dismissal in the Marquess of Grolier's voice was clear to all. "I'll not marry your granddaughter now."

"You signed a binding contract," the old duke hissed.

The stranger who stood next to Benjamin lifted a hand. "Excuse me, Your Grace. Actually, the marquess didn't."

"Who are you?" the Marquess of Grolier asked.

"Mr. Edward Black, Mr. Hollandale's solicitor." The man smiled sheepishly. "I'm one of many he has on retainer to help him run his businesses."

"More proof he's a man of trade," her grandfather muttered.

The solicitor pushed his spectacles over the bridge of his nose. "The reason it's not a contract is Miss Worsley never agreed to the marriage in the first place. You cannot offer something you have no right to. She's of age. She doesn't need permission to marry. And the Duke of Exehill doesn't own an estate with a horse farm.

"Exehill, listen to what is happening here," Grolier sighed heavily. "Your granddaughter is in love with another man. She had no idea that you'd arranged this marriage." He narrowed his eyes. "You've wasted my time like you did my father." The marquess turned to Celeste. "If I'd known, I would not have signed that marital settlement, no matter what estate he offered. I apologize if I've caused you or Mr. Hollandale any distress."

"Your father?" Pelham asked.

Grolier nodded. "After my mother passed away, Exehill tried to arrange a marriage between my father and Miss Worsley's mother. But it never came to fruition as her mother married another."

The man was a pawn in her grandfather's scheme, the same as she was. She had to find out the truth about what her grandfather had offered. "Lord Grolier, could you tell me about the estate he promised you in exchange for your land?"

The marquess slid a side-eyed glance to her grandfather, then shook his head. "Besides your hand in marriage, I was to receive a small estate in Essex with an extensive stable of superior racing horseflesh.

"Was the name of the estate Blackberry Abbey?" Malcolm asked.

The marquess nodded.

Her knees threatened to buckle as she realized what her grandfather had done. It didn't make any difference if she had married Lord Grolier or not. Her grandfather had planned to bankrupt her parents and give their farm and estate to the marquess. She kept her gaze down, praying her tears wouldn't fall. All those years of trying to please her grandfather had been for naught. Completely wasted.

And she would never be able to make up for all that time. How many times had her grandfather broken her heart, yet she'd remained loyal? Her throat tightened, and a solitary tear fell to the ground. No one could see it, but the damage had been done. She'd been naïve to hope that her grandfather would reconcile with her parents, let alone forgive the mortgage.

"Darling, Your parents owe your grandfather nothing. Mr. Black has verified it." Malcolm wrapped his arm around hers, his strength keeping her from falling in a heap. "He can't hurt you or them anymore."

"Indeed, I can," her grandfather countered. "My granddaughter stole priceless silver teaspoons from me. The housekeeper saw it and had the gel followed. She went to your house *unchaperoned*." He pointed at Malcolm as he raised his voice loud enough that the crowd scooted closer to hear every scandalous word. "She left without the teaspoons." He cocked his head with a malevolent smile. "I'll have you thrown in Newgate for this. We'll see how your army of legal minds deal with you being transported."

She wanted to scream and rant at the man who was supposedly her own flesh and blood. How dare he try to turn his ploy of claiming Alice was a thief on Malcolm? She would go to Newgate herself before allowing her Malcolm to step foot in that place.

"That's a lie," Celeste hissed in her grandfather's direction.

"Celeste," Malcolm soothed.

She turned to Malcolm, praying he'd forgive her for dragging him into this scandal. Tears burned her cheeks, but she refused to be silent. "He's evil and a privileged fop who cares for nothing except his precious legacy. I'm sorry you're involved with this...."

He wiped away a tear that stood suspended on her cheek.

"I'm sorry you're involved with me," she murmured.

Just then, Benjamin tapped Malcolm on the shoulder and whispered. Malcolm's gaze didn't move from hers as he listened.

She waited for Malcolm's expression to dissolve into disgust as he studied her. If fate were kind, the ground would open and swallow her whole. At least she could lick her wounds in private. She didn't give a whit if all of London society heard the mad tale of her grandfather's machinations, but it was unbearable to be in Malcolm's presence. None of this would have happened if he'd stayed away from her.

Malcolm nodded once, then turned to Exehill with a ruthless gleam in his gaze. "Respectfully, *Your Grace*, you're telling a falsehood. I do not know where your teaspoons are, nor does your granddaughter."

She didn't move as Malcolm stared straight at her grandfather. He had to be bluffing. Otherwise, it made no sense for him to say such a thing. He'd told her he'd put the teaspoons in his iron lockbox to keep them safe.

"A solution to this quandary," Pelham announced as he held up one finger, then pointed at the solicitor. "I'll accompany Exehill home along with Mr. Black. If the teaspoons are not there, we'll make haste to Hollandale's laboratory and investigate."

The solicitor nodded his agreement.

Benjamin stepped forward. "Your Grace," he addressed Pelham. "Since it's my wife that the Duke of Exehill has insulted, I insist that I go with Mr. Black. If the teaspoons aren't there, I can escort everyone to Mr. Hollandale's workshop."

Pelham nodded. "A sound plan."

Celeste's grandfather's mouth was gaping wide like a fish suddenly finding itself out of water.

"Come, Exehill." Pelham took his arm like a child about to be punished for a misdeed. "I don't have all night. My sisters are attending this soiree, and I promised them both a dance."

"I shall accompany you," Malcolm said, but his cynical gaze still bored into her grandfather's shocked face. "Mr. Black, once the teaspoons are found, shall we see what legal action we can have the barristers pursue? Defamation, slander, and false statements to harm another come to mind."

"I'll come with you." She would never forgive herself if her grandfather pulled some trick that would endanger Malcolm. "My place is by your side."

Malcolm glanced down at her. His eyes softened with tenderness. "I want you safe."

Ravenscroft shook his head. "Do not go to his house. You should stay with Miss Worsley." He glanced at the crowd gathered around them, then lowered his voice. "Or take her away from here. This scandal will be on everyone's tongue."

Pelham turned his back on Celeste's grandfather, then took Celeste's hand. "I'm sorry but what Ravenscroft suggests is best for you both."

Trafford had also come forward, then frowned. "She can't go home. I don't trust what Exehill will do." He glanced over her shoulder. "Ravenscroft's mother is here, but his great aunt is home. She would be a suitable chaperone."

Ravenscroft rolled his eyes with a smile. "Have you met my Aunt Edith? Chaperoning is not one of her fortes."

"I agree with Ravenscroft," Malcolm said. "I should not let her out of my sight. Exehill will not be happy after this evening. I don't trust him not to take his anger out on Celeste." He turned to her. "Agreed?"

She nodded, thankful he was looking out for her. "He's never done it before, but I've never seen him so adamant about my acquiescence."

"It's settled then." Pelham nodded, then turned to her grandfather, who was practically shouting at Mr. Black. The solicitor stood there stone-faced, allowing her grandfather to threaten and bluster to his heart's content.

Malcolm placed his hand on her lower back. "Come, love," he murmured so the crowd couldn't hear. "My driver is waiting in the mews for us. I know a way through the side of the house that will allow us to escape everyone's curious eyes."

"Malcolm?"

He stopped and turned to her. She lifted her hand to soothe the lines of anger on his brow, then lowered it slowly, without making contact. She'd wait until they were alone to touch her beloved. No need to add fuel to the rumors that were undoubtedly spreading like wildfires. The crowd would still be discussing such a spectacle tomorrow in all the drawing rooms during the social calls.

"Do you know where the teaspoons are?" she asked softly.

"Not here," he said gruffly, then took her hand.

In minutes, they were speeding through the streets toward the opposite side of Mayfair. As soon as they had entered the carriage, Malcolm held her, his warmth comforting. She buried her head against his neck, and he pulled her tighter against him. "Never again," he breathed. "Never again shall the man have anything to do with you."

"The idea that he could hurt you is something I'll always be fearful of." She held tight. In the carriage, they were in their own world. With each block that they traveled, the threatening feeling of danger ebbed.

"He can't hurt me." Malcolm pressed his lips to hers. "With the help of Marianne,

Benjamin returned the teaspoons to their rightful place."

"What?" She leaned back and studied his eyes. "How?"

"After you warned Alice, she went straight to Benjamin. They went to see Marianne, who let Benjamin in the house and took him to the pantry where the silver was kept. She had the key to the silver pantry." He smiled and tucked a stray lock of her hair behind her ear, his touch gentle like she was a rare piece of china.

"So, there's no chance Exehill will be able to make good on his promise to have you charged with theft?" It was the first time she'd ever referred to her grandfather by his ducal title. She would never again claim him as her kin.

"None," Malcolm said, pressing another gentle kiss against her mouth.

"Where are we going?"

"To our home."

CHAPTER FIFTEEN

M alcolm was careful as they arrived at his Mayfair mansion. Because it was a massive neo-classical structure, it was something that most people slowed their walk or carriage ride to gawk over. With massive iron gates guarding the drive, it was easy for Malcolm to lock out the outside world when need be, and that's what was called for tonight. With her by his side, he would do anything and every- thing to protect her from further gossip. Tonight's crowd would ensure that Exehill's actions would be dissected ad nauseum in all the London drawing rooms tomorrow.

Because of Exehill's actions tonight, he'd put Celeste right in the bull's-eye of scandal. But Malcolm would protect her the best he could. She would stay with him tonight since she couldn't return to the duke's home. They'd keep it a secret until he could secure a common license. It was best that they marry quickly to squelch the rampant rumors over her grandfather's action tonight. Reluctantly, he knew she'd have to stay somewhere else tomorrow or her reputation would be guaranteed to be in tatters.

Malcolm leaned out the window as soon as the carriage gently rocked to and fro, indicating they were on his drive. "Drive to the servants' entrance, Jack."

The coachman tipped his hat. "Of course, Mr. Hollandale."

As soon as the carriage came to a stop, Malcolm tugged the hood of Celeste's cloak over her head. "In case someone is watching." He dipped his head and pressed a kiss to her lips. "Hungry."

"Not for food," she murmured, then worried her lower lip with her teeth.

He smiled as his cock twitched to attention. "We think the same." He knocked on the roof, and immediately, a footman opened the door. Malcolm exited and held out his hand to assist Celeste.

Without hesitating, she put her hand in his and gracefully stepped to the ground.

"May this be the first of thousands of times that I assist the love of my life as she exits our carriage." He brought her hand to his lips, then wrapped his arms around her waist. "Come, darling."

"What will your servants think of me?" Celeste came to a stop and peeked from under her cloak.

"They'll think their mistress is finally home," he said the words with a certainty that he'd found his perfect wife and would never let her go.

As soon as they arrived at the back entrance, his housekeeper, Mrs. Morris, and his butler, Mr. Simon, greeted them at the door.

"John, the footman, rushed home and told us what had happened," Mrs. Morris clucked gently. "Miss Worsley, I have a hot bath and a tray waiting for you." She dipped a brief curtsey. "If you'll follow me," the housekeeper invited with a slight smile. "It's good to have you here."

Malcolm felt a breath of relief at the sight of Celeste's smile.

"I would like that, Mrs. Morris." She turned to him, then hesitated.

He could tell by the way she searched his face, she didn't know how much she could say in front of his servants. So, he bent down and whispered for her ears only. "I'll come find you after I have my bath."

Mrs. Morris didn't wait for Celeste to reply. Instead, she waved her arm for Celeste to precede her. Malcolm watched her walk through his house until she disappeared from view.

Mr. Simon rocked back on his heels with a satisfied grin. "I hope it's acceptable, but I put Miss Worsley in the duchess's apartments."

"Thank you." His home used to belong to the Duke of Takeley, who needed the money to pay off his debt to Pelham. Malcolm had completely redecorated it, including the duchess's apartments next to his.

"I've sent the Macalester boys to the Duke of Exehill's house to retrieve her clothing. They'll not say where she's staying."

"You've thought of everything," Malcolm said.

"We all have been waiting for this, sir. And I didn't want the lady of the house to feel any discomfort. Mrs. Morris and I also took it upon ourselves to send for a dressing gown and all the accompaniments from Mademoiselle Mignon's shop." He leaned a bit closer to Malcolm and lowered his voice. "Mademoiselle Mignon is the most popular modiste in all of London. Nothing is too good for the soon-to-be bride of yours, sir."

Chuckling, Malcolm shook his head as he made his

way to his own apartments for a bath. He wasn't the only one anxious for Celeste to become his bride. The entire staff welcomed her, and Malcolm was thankful for that. He wanted Celeste to fall in love with this place and the people who worked there.

After he undressed, Malcolm dismissed Robert, his valet. A large tub built to accommodate his long legs sat in front of the fireplace at the end of the room. The flames provided enough light to make the steam rising from the warm bath visible. Malcolm slipped into the tub without wasting another minute. His staff was remarkable. Robert had even set out a glass of whisky to sip on as he soaked in the water.

As he relaxed in the hot water, Malcolm pushed all the wretchedness over the last several days out of his mind. Grolier showed himself to be a decent human being who had understood what Celeste's grandfather had done and had bowed out gracefully. Tomorrow, Malcolm would send a note inviting him to call upon him at his work. If the man needed help or a friend, then Malcolm would do everything he could to help him.

He took a sip of whisky, then rested his arm on the rim of the tub, allowing the glass to dangle from his fingers. He hadn't had the chance to finish his work on the varnish and wouldn't have any time to spare before opening night. Frankly, his mind wasn't even thinking about it. He had other priorities, namely Celeste. He wanted her settled as soon as possible.

He dunked his head under the water, then slowly rose. A little meow sounded beside him. One stood on her hind legs, desperate to catch the reflecting prisms that danced on the carpet from the cut glass he held in his hand.

"How did you get here, little one?" he murmured as he straightened in the tub. At the sound of the water slapping against the sides, the white kitten forgot all about the prisms and stood at attention, studying him.

"I let her in," a sultry voice sounded behind him.

When he turned, his breath caught at the sight of his duchess before him. Wearing a cream-colored dressing gown that left nothing to the imagination, Celeste gracefully walked to him.

All thoughts of work instantly disappeared. His entire body tightened at the sight of Celeste standing just a few yards away.

"Come closer."

She came to stand before the fire, the silk turning translucent and showcasing the outline of her luscious body. "I thought you had taken the kitten back to the workshop."

Malcolm finished the last of his whisky. "She wanted to stay here to await your arrival," he teased.

"Malcolm," she playfully scolded.

"Can I help that she and I want the same thing?" His grin slowly faded, and his gaze ate up the distance between them. He itched to make love to her and then proclaim to the world that she was his. No man could love her as he would.

He wanted this woman more than he wanted anything else in his life before.

"Thank you for this." She waved a hand down the floral silk dressing gown. "It's beautiful. I feel like a princess."

"You're beautiful, and my duchess."

She bit her lip and smiled. "Do you need help bathing?" Her voice dropped into a low, seductive whisper, a siren song just for him. One he could not and would not resist.

His heart boomed like thunder as he instantly understood her offer. "Are you volunteering?" He ached for her, and if she were going to offer herself, he would abide by her wishes.

A wave of his hand invited her closer, and he watched with bated breath as she stepped forward, the emerald depths of her eyes deepening into a hue that reminded him of malachite, a fitting description. The ancient Egyptians claimed the stone represented the afterlife and resurrection. His and Celeste's lives had been forever changed due to her grandfather's disgrace and had become stronger regardless of the scandal. Now, they were beginning a new life together.

"Allow me to be your valet this evening." She picked up the linen toweling from the chair nearby, her eyes dancing over his dripping body in unmistakable hunger. He stood slowly, searching her face as his arousal strained with her proximity. Celeste's gaze skittered hungrily down his length before she stepped closer with an eagerness that fanned his own desire.

As soon as she slowly stroked the towel over his chest, he lifted his arms wide to give her greater access. "It seems I'm wet for you, duchess. Are you the same for me?" His voice grew low as he whispered the words.

The pulse at the base of her neck thundered wildly as he awaited her answer.

"Yes. You have me in a state of utter chaos."

"Chaos?" he growled playfully.

"Chaos…ecstasy." Her hands trembled as she spoke, the only sign that his seductive siren wasn't entirely in control of her emotions. "It's the same feeling. I can't escape it, and I don't want to."

He slid his fingers beneath her chin and stared into her eyes. "It is for me, too." He leaned near and crushed his mouth to hers, tasting her with an intensity that made his heart race. Her hands locked around his neck as a wave of pleasure coursed through his body. He stepped out of the water and grabbed another towel to dry himself, careful not to disturb the lingering heat between them.

She didn't tear her gaze from his body. The hungry appreciation in her eyes ignited his own desire.

The kitten's soft snore enveloped the room in a blanket of peace, and he smiled with satisfaction. Quickly, he scooped Celeste into his arms, pressing his naked body against her warmth. "Do you want me as much as I want you?" he murmured close to her ear before dragging his teeth along the skin of her neck.

She lifted her head to give him better access. "Always." She coiled her arms around his neck and clung tightly to him.

In ten quick strides, he had her at his bed. He leaned over her, studying every beautiful inch of her body.

"This is the second time I've asked you this question." He waggled his eyebrows. "I'm hopeful for the right answer this time. Celeste, will you do me the honor of marrying me?" His gaze studied her face for any hesitation.

His beautiful duchess smiled, making her even more beautiful in his eyes. "Yes. If I didn't make myself clear, then a thousand and one times, yes."

"Thank God," he said as relief poured through him.

She pulled him near, then raked her fingers through his hair. The groaning rumble of a growl echoed low in his chest, and blood pounded in his ears. He searched her eyes for any hesitation and found none. From the first moment he saw her, he knew she would be different. She was passionate, honest, and forthright.

"I always knew it would be like this with you."

He brushed a silken lock of hair behind her ear. "What do you mean?"

"You make me feel cherished." She released a tremulous breath. "I vow to do the same for you every day we have together on this earth. I love you," she whispered. Her hand crept to his cheek as if drawn by an invisible wire. Her eyelids drooped slightly, and a sultry smile spread across her face. She nuzzled against him.

"I love you." There and then, he knew that he'd give his life for the woman he held in his arms.

She moved her lips to his. In concert, he bracketed his arms around her head again, protecting her while careful not to crush her. She brushed her mouth once, twice against his before she licked his lower lip.

"You taste of whisky."

"Is it offensive?" I can clean my teeth—"

Without warning, she licked his lips again. "I love the taste of it." She blinked slowly. "I love the taste of you."

He was the one who lowered his mouth to hers. He licked her lips. She opened on a sensual moan, and his tongue swept in and caressed hers. Unable to deny himself, he pressed his hard length against her softness. She spread her legs, encouraging him to touch her deeper.

His hands roamed over her ribs, finding the ties that held her dressing gown closed and gradually untying them until one side was completely exposed.

Celeste never looked away as she encouraged him to explore further by pushing away the fabric and baring her breasts to him.

"Touch me," she pleaded, cupping her breasts as if offering them to him. It was the most erotic sight he'd ever seen. He lowered his mouth to one breast and sucked her nipple into his mouth. She took his hand, guiding it to her other breast. She arched into his touch, a silent request for more.

He was hers to rule. Pleasure was his only task. He sucked her nipple and she mewled in pleasure as he rolled the other between his thumb and forefinger. All he wanted was to please her and explore every inch of her glorious body.

He slowed and braced himself on his elbows. By then, she was panting, hungry for more. He moved down her body, kissing her every inch of the way, exploring every curve and softness he could find until he reached her hips and finally her curls.

He lifted himself off the bed and knelt on the floor. He pulled her to the edge of the mattress and spread her legs. His duchess watched every move. Delicately, he parted her folds with his fingertips and tasted her fully with his tongue. Celeste watched as he flicked his tongue rapidly against her most sensitive spot. She quivered beneath him with each stroke. Wanting to give her more, he entered her with his tongue, savoring every delicious inch of her.

"Malcolm," she moaned. "Please."

He did as asked, slowly swirling his tongue around the tender, swollen nub. She was a banquet, and he was a starving man. She was as sweet as ambrosia, and he'd never tire of bringing her to climax as he devoured her.

He tasted her with a flick of his tongue, then licked her hard before sucking her clitoris into his mouth. She tightened her fists in his hair with each swirl of his tongue. The pain of her pulling his hair ratcheted up his own desire. Unable to bear it, he fisted his cock. His essence covered the crown. It wouldn't take much for him to come, but this night wasn't about him. It was about her, the love of his life.

As he continued to work her with his tongue, he slid

one finger inside her before adding another. She bucked slightly under him. When he added a third finger, he sucked her nub hard. It was enough to unleash an almighty scream of pleasure from her.

He stood, then covered her with his body. His knees were between her legs as he kissed her deep and long. He wanted her to taste the pleasure that he'd feasted upon. He deepened the kiss and moaned. Just tasting her made him want to come. As his tongue tangled with hers, he slid his cock through her drenched folds. She lifted her hips and wrapped her legs around his waist.

He slid inside, then stilled, burying his head into the elegant curve of her neck. He was home, and he never wanted to leave. But the urge to chase his own pleasure became overpowering. Her muscles still contracted from her orgasm, squeezing his cock. He pumped into her once, twice, then let go. When his seed flooded her, he stilled, savoring every moment of holding her.

He pressed a kiss to her neck and sighed her name.

She held him close with one hand as her other fingered the locks of his hair.

"I must be crushing you."

She held him tight, refusing to let him get off her. "I want you near. It helps me forget the ugliness from earlier this evening."

Slowly, he slid to one side of her, then rolled until she was lying on him. "It's over. I'm certain a note will be waiting for us that the teaspoons are safely ensconced in your grandfather's house."

She placed her fingers against his mouth. "As of tonight he's no longer my grandfather. He's simply Exehill."

As she rested her chin on his chest, he searched her

gaze. There was no hurt or dismay, just resignation. "I'm sorry, darling, for how things turned out."

"I'm not." She smiled and pressed a kiss to his mouth. "Now, I have the man of my dreams."

"That's a fair point, as I have the woman of my dreams." He played with a lock of her hair, but his gaze still held hers. "Would a common license suffice for marrying me?"

"As long as it's the quickest way, I'm fine with it." She tilted her head. "They cost a couple of pounds, correct? I have that amount."

"I think I can afford the expense." He laughed and placed a kiss to her forehead. "Before you, I would have been embarrassed that I wasn't able to buy a special license since I'm not of the aristocracy."

She snuggled a little closer. "Titles mean nothing to me. It's the person who counts. I fell in love with you. You've taught me it's all right to put myself first."

Just then, One climbed up the covers and circled until she was close to Celeste. "There's my darling," she cooed.

"I thought I was your darling," he countered with a teasing lilt of outrage.

"Hush," she crooned as she played with the hair on his chest. "I always have room for both of you in my bed." She bit her lip with a smile. "But you are the one I will always hold in my arms."

He tenderly kissed her, then pulled her close. "As long as I'm in your arms, I don't care where we are. As long as I'm with you, I'm home."

CHAPTER SIXTEEN

C eleste opened her eyes, then blinked twice. At first, it was hard to reconcile where she was. Then all the events of yesterday tumbled into her musings. She smiled and closed her eyes and relived the sweet memories of Malcolm making love to her. After he'd taken her the first time, they'd made love three more times.

The man was insatiable. He couldn't seem to get enough of her.

She felt the same about him. All through the night, she had to touch him. One hand stroke would lead to a kiss, then another. Soon, they were making love again. No longer did she feel invisible. When Malcolm caressed her, held her, or kissed her, he ensured she knew how vital she was to him.

He made her feel beautiful.

A quiet purr rumbled beside her. One was fast asleep. Celeste reached over and gently petted the top of her head. "We have to come up with a better name for you, my darling."

The kitten's head popped up.

"You want to be called Darling?" As soon as she asked, the kitten stretched, then rubbed her head against Celeste. "All right then. Darling, it is."

A knock sounded on the door, and Marianne popped her head inside. "Good morning, Miss." She stepped inside and closed the door. "I've come to help you dress. A tray will be delivered shortly."

"I'm starved." Celeste stretched her arms over her head.

"I can imagine after the night you had."

Celeste turned to stare at her maid, but she was busy tending to the fire. There had been nothing judgmental in Marianne's tone. Perhaps Celeste was being a little prickly about the matter, but there was little doubt that the *ton* would make mincemeat of her and Malcolm as time passed. While a common license meant they only had to wait a week, those seven days could feel like an eternity if their scandal was the juiciest rumor within society.

"You must be wondering why I'm in Mr. Hollandale's bed." Celeste waited for Marianne to turn.

"Not really. If I had a handsome and kind man who treated me like a queen, I'd be in his bed too." Marianne nodded as a knock sounded. Without hesitating, the maid answered the door. "Come in, Mrs. Morris," Marianne chirped.

Celeste's cheeks felt hotter than a smithy's fire. It was one thing to be discovered in Malcolm's bed by Marianne. It was quite another when it was the housekeeper. She wanted to dive under the covers.

"Good morning, Miss Worsley," Mrs. Morris said with a smile as she placed a breakfast tray on the table near the bed. "Mr. Simon and I had your clothes delivered here. I hope you don't mind." She looked at Marianne and nodded. "You'll make a fine addition here, Marianne. I don't need to tell you how to prepare Miss Worsley for the day."

"Thank you, Mrs. Morris." Marianne continued to lay out Celeste's clothes. "I think you should wear your new silk gown. The pink one."

"But that is more of a gown for a formal event," Celeste murmured.

"Speaking of which," Mrs. Morris said as she turned her gaze to Celeste. "Might I suggest you eat quickly and get dressed, ma'am? Your parents await you downstairs." She beamed, then lowered her voice. "So is Mr. Hollandale. I've never seen him this happy before. And I've been working for him for over eight years." She glanced around the room and nodded once in satisfaction. "I'll leave you in Marianne's capable hands and tell his lordship and her ladyship that you'll be down shortly." She shimmied her shoulders. "I love company. It gives a whole new meaning to serving."

Completely bemused, Celeste asked, "My parents are here? Whatever for?"

But Mrs. Morris didn't answer.

As soon as the door closed, Marianne turned to the tray and lifted the lid. "You should eat a little something before you go down. While you do that, I'll prepare the bath for you in the duchess's apartment."

Without another word, Marianne swept through Malcolm's bedroom and into the attached duchess apartment as if she'd been here for years instead of one day.

After half an hour, wearing her pink silk gown and matching shoes, Celeste walked to the salon attached to Malcolm's study. She'd only been here once before but recalled where it was. Anything to do with Malcolm she had memorized.

Her stomach fluttered in excitement about seeing her parents, but it could only mean that the rumors must have somehow reached Blackberry Abbey overnight.

She smoothed her hand down her midriff. There was only one way to handle the scandal, and that was to address it head-on. She took a breath for courage, then knocked on the door as she entered.

She came to a dead stop. Malcolm and her parents were raising a toast to one another.

"What's going on?" she asked.

Immediately, all three heads turned.

"Celeste, my darling girl," her mother called out as she rushed to her side. She took Celeste in her arms and kissed both cheeks. "You are radiant."

Her father had joined them, hugged Celeste, and kissed her cheek. "Hello, sweetheart."

As she hugged her father, Celeste glanced at Malcolm. "What's going on?" she mouthed.

"Your parents came as quickly as they could to help you and me." By then, he was by her side. "Come, let's all sit down."

"There's a tea tray prepared." Her mother turned to Celeste. "Have you eaten?"

Celeste sat on a sofa in the seating area. "Yes, I had a cup of tea and a cherry tart upstairs."

Her mother smoothed her skirts, then sat on the opposite sofa. Her father took the seat next to her mother. Malcolm sat next to Celeste and took her hand, bringing it to his mouth. "Good morning, love."

He said it so softly that only she could hear it. "Good morning."

"Malcolm, you'll have to watch Celeste in the mornings. She sometimes doesn't eat enough. She ends up being famished by midday."

Not releasing her hand, Malcolm nodded. "I shall remember that, my lady. Have no fear. Your daughter is in the best of hands."

Her mother beamed at Malcolm.

Her father nodded in approval. "Exactly what we want to hear, Hollandale."

"Mother and Father," Celeste exclaimed with a laugh. "What are you about?"

"Well, if you're to be married, he needs to know your vices." Her mother chuckled and took Celeste's father's hand in hers. "Malcolm has certainly regaled us with a list of your virtues."

Her father brought her hand to his mouth just as Malcolm had done to her. "Indeed. I think it bodes well for their marriage. Don't you think it as well, Susan?"

"You were just like that when you were courting me." Her mother blushed.

"And now?" Her father arched one of his eyebrows.

"You're ten times worse," her mother answered.

"Or ten times better, depending upon how you look at it." Her father relaxed, placed his hand around his wife's shoulders, and brought her close.

"What are you both doing here?" Celeste sat on the edge of her seat. "If it's about last night—"

Her mother shook her head. "Malcolm sent for us. We didn't hear about that until Malcolm informed us about my father's behavior." She glanced at her husband and then turned to Celeste. "I'm sorry, darling, that you went through all that with him."

Her father pressed a kiss to her mother's temple, then turned to her and Malcolm. "We could not allow you to marry a stranger for Exehill's benefit. I always doubted if he'd allow us to pay off our debt."

"What do you mean?" Malcolm squeezed Celeste's hand. "Exehill repeatedly told Celeste that he'd forgive the mortgage if she married the man he chose."

Her mother smiled sadly. "I think he wanted us indebted to him. But we wanted you to spend time with him. When my mother was alive, she kept him in good humor. But after she died, he and I always fought. We were like water and oil. We thought you might form a bond with him that neither your father nor I could manage." She glanced at Celeste's father and smiled slightly. "We hoped he might relinquish his harsh stand when he came to know you." She turned to Celeste. Her eyes shined with unshed tears. "How could we be such horrible people if we produced a child such as you, beautiful inside and out?"

"Oh, Mother." Tears gathered in her eyes. "I feel the same about you both."

"Your Malcolm…" Her father choked on the words.

Celeste leaned forward at such a sight. She'd never seen her loving father so emotional. "Father?"

"It's all right," he said softly, then cleared his throat. "Your Malcolm was a godsend when he paid off the mortgage. I don't know what I would have done."

"Darling, you don't have to do this," her mother said gently.

"I do, Susan. I've kept my tongue for too long regarding that man." He turned his gaze to her and Malcolm. The redness in his eyes betrayed the emotion that her father never liked to reveal. "He never thought I could care and provide for your mother and you." He stared at his hand entangled with her mother's fingers. "I let it go on for far too long. I should have confronted him earlier, but you lived with him, and I wanted you to have your Season. You deserved that and so much more." He raised his gaze to Malcolm, then to Celeste. "I should have never allowed you to live with him. You've paid too high a price."

Celeste went to her father and hugged him. "Don't say that." She kissed him and then her mother on their cheeks. She returned to Malcolm's side and took his hand in hers. "I'm grateful for the time that I stayed with him. Otherwise, I wouldn't have met the love of my life."

Malcolm smiled and pulled her close. "I feel the same."

Her mother's sadness evaporated slowly. "I never thought of it that way, but you're right."

Her stoic father was quiet for a moment, then he nodded. "Indeed. I'm glad too. Though I'm thankful that the mortgage is no more, I'm more thankful that my daughter has found a wonderful, giving man to marry." His brow furrowed. "If I have to give my Celeste up, I'm glad she's with you, Hollandale."

"Hear, hear," her mother called out joyfully.

After everyone laughed, her father reached across the space and shook Malcolm's hand. "I promise to pay back the mortgage. I never missed a payment to Exehill, and I plan the same with you."

"The truth is, sir, that I consider you my family. I certainly will be when I marry your daughter." Malcolm never allowed his gaze to leave her father's. "I will not take your money. Family looks out for family."

"Thank you." Her father returned Malcolm's smile and then turned to Celeste. "So, you want to marry this man?"

Celeste turned to Malcolm with a smile she knew had to be overflowing with joy. "It's my greatest wish."

"Excellent." Before her mother could continue, Mr.

Simon knocked and entered the room. "Mr. Merknight has arrived, sir."

Malcolm glanced at the longcase clock in the room. "A tad early, but I'm happy. The sooner I can marry my duchess, the better."

"Now?" Celeste asked. "What about a common license?"

Her father waggled his eyebrows. "Your mother and I thought it best that you do not wait, especially after what happened yesterday. So, I took Hollandale to Doctor's Commons this morning and explained to the archbishop that my daughter needed to marry quickly. He and I went to university together." He smiled mischievously. "Sometimes, being a viscount does have its advantages."

Celeste turned to Malcolm. "You did?"

"If it's acceptable to you. We could marry now." His smile was brighter than the midday sun. "I sent for the vicar who married Alice and Benjamin. He said he'd be delighted to marry us."

Once again, the man before her had surprised her with the loveliest gift. That meant they could start their life together that very day. She clasped his hand to her heart. "I don't know what to say except yes. Yes!" She laughed as she gazed into his eyes. "If I wasn't clear enough, the answer is yes."

Mr. Simon escorted the vicar into the room. When Celeste's parents rose to greet him, Malcolm brought Celeste into his arms as the others looked on and whispered, "After we marry, I planned for your parents to visit Lady Ravenscroft. She's going to reintroduce them to society. Your parents don't want to be under your grandfather's shadow anymore."

"You think of everything." She pulled away slightly

and kissed her soon-to-be husband's cheek. "Have I told you that I love you?"

"Not today," he whispered against her lips. "Would it be remiss of me if I said that you don't do it often enough?" he asked teasingly.

When he pulled away, his smile stole her breath. It promised all sorts of pleasure was in her future. She had no doubt it would start today and always be a part of their lives together. "What shall we do while they're gone?" she asked in the same low tone.

Malcolm smiled against her ear. "We're spending the rest of the day in bed."

"Oh, I like the way you think, Mr. Hollandale."

"Anything for you, duchess." He pressed a quick kiss on her lips. "I love you."

"That's enough of that," her father said with a laugh.

Malcolm pulled her close and turned to her father. "Respectfully, sir, I believe there is never enough of that, especially when I'm with your daughter." He turned his blazing smile in her direction. "Are you ready to marry me?"

"I've been ready to marry you my whole life." Celeste wrapped her arm around his.

Malcolm escorted them all to the formal salon, where several chairs had been lined up and guests were already waiting for the ceremony to begin. The Duke of Pelham smiled and nodded their way. Lord Ravenscroft and Lord Trafford also smiled when they entered the room. Celeste's friends, Lady Honoria, Lady Pippa, and Lady Amelia Windhorst, were in attendance and waved, wearing wide smiles on their faces. But Alice and Benjamin's broad grins and hugs nearly brought her to tears.

"I can't believe you're here," Celeste whispered to Alice.

"Mr. Hollandale asked if we could attend," Alice answered, beaming.

Malcolm slid up next to them. "Darling, if it would be acceptable to you, I thought Benjamin and Alice could be our witnesses. Just as we were for them."

"I would like that very much." Celeste's eyes filled with tears. "Why does the happiest day of my life make me cry?"

"Because you, my duchess, are as amazed as me that we have such wonderful and supporting friends and family around us."

Celeste nodded and squeezed his hand. "You know what this means, don't you?"

Malcolm shook his head. "Tell me."

"It means you'll have to hire my lady's maid again." Celeste grinned, then winked at him.

When Malcolm threw his head back and laughed, Celeste joined in.

"Just as long as you come with her to live in my home. Now, it's time to start, my sweet duchess," Malcolm whispered, then led Celeste to the front of the room.

As the vicar had them repeat their vows, an overwhelming gratitude filled Celeste. She loved this wonderful man to whom she was pledging her troth. And not a doubt existed in her head that he also loved her. Only with him by her side did she learn that thinking and acting for her own benefit was perfectly acceptable. He would ensure that she remembered that valuable lesson. And she vowed always to remind him that he was the best of men, and she was a lucky bride to be the one who could call him husband.

After the announcement that they were husband and wife, Malcolm leaned down and pressed his lips to hers in a kiss that promised his fealty and love forever.

When he pulled away to the cheers of friends and family, she said for his hearing only. "I love you today and promise I'll love you more tomorrow."

"I love you," he murmured, never taking his eyes from hers. "You'll always have my heart, my darling duchess."

EPILOGUE

The excitement of opening night at the Drury Lane Theatre was palpable. The buzz of conversations ebbed and flowed as time wore on. Laughter and the discordance of instruments warming up in the orchestra added a certain exhilaration. Malcolm knew a thing or two about exhilaration and elation. He'd been in a perpetual state of each since last week when he and his beautiful wife had married.

As he glanced around his box, it was a different experience tonight. Every other time when he'd sat here at the theatre, it was pleasant but not anything that interested him unless Miss Celeste Worsley had been sitting in the box next to his, which her grandfather owned. She'd sit tall and act uninterested in anything other than the play. But Malcolm would constantly steal glances her way where she sat in all her glory, looking down her nose at him.

He chuckled to himself how they'd both had such startling differences of opinion about one another until the last time they were here together. Thankfully, they no longer hid their true natures and feelings for each other.

Malcolm leaned near Celeste. The urge to touch her never diminished. If anything, it had only increased since they'd exchanged their vows.

Unable to stop himself, he stared at Celeste's profile as she talked to her parents. How could his wife—how he relished calling her that—become more beautiful every day? They'd been together practically every hour since they'd married, eating, bathing, sleeping—though little of that occurred—had consumed their days.

Her parents were staying with them until the end of the week. He'd had the opportunity to talk to Lord Worsley several times, and he was an honorable man. He was successful as a horse breeder and an astute man of business. The fire had strewn misfortune in the path of Celeste's parents' future, but Celeste's father never complained as he rebuilt their wealth.

He and Celeste only saw her parents in the evenings as they'd had a full social schedule since their return to London. They spent the majority of their time with Lady Ravenscroft. She'd been instrumental to Lord and Lady Worsley's acceptance back into the *ton*.

Which had been a blessing. He and his duchess had surrounded themselves in a cocoon filled with laughter, earnest conversations about their hopes and dreams for their futures, and, of course, lovemaking.

"What's caused that expression?" Under the disguise of straightening his cravat, Celeste reached up and caressed his neck and shoulder. The high color in her cheeks betrayed her excitement at touching him.

"I'm a besotted fool and am very proud of it," he whispered.

"Then I am one as well, sir." She laughed softly, then bit her lip. She glanced at him through half-lowered lids, knowing that it would drive him wild to have her.

"At intermission, I might have to find an empty room and ravish you," he murmured, coming close enough to kiss her but never taking his eyes from hers.

She smoothed her hands down his lapels. "Do you think it will always be like this between us?"

"I promise," he said tenderly, then winked at her. "Even when I'm a tottering fool who takes an hour to chase you around our bedroom." He took her hand and squeezed.

"I quite like the sound of that." She glanced over his shoulder. "Lord Grolier is here."

"I invited him." When she looked at him in surprise, Malcolm shrugged one shoulder. "I know what it feels like to be an outsider. I thought to at least offer friendship. He was quite civil about giving you up. I would never have done that."

"You are incorrigible." She pushed him gently. "Bring him here so I may introduce him to my parents."

He squeezed her waist affectionately. The need to touch her constantly never wavered, and it was an affliction he hoped never to be cured of.

When he made his way to Grolier, he extended his hand. "Welcome, Grolier. Celeste and I are delighted you could join us this evening."

Grolier shook his hand in return. "Thank you for inviting me." The man smiled warmly. "And congratulations on your marriage."

"Thank you." Malcolm grinned.

Grolier didn't let go of his hand. "I am sincere about my felicitations that she married you. She deserved happiness after having to deal with Exehill."

They both looked at the duke's empty box. He and Celeste hadn't heard a word from him since it announced that they were married. Perhaps the old goat was still upset that she'd gotten her wish and married a "man of trade."

Grolier nodded toward the stage. "That's rather odd. Actors are appearing on the stage and then running back to hide behind the curtain."

When Malcolm turned his attention to the stage, he saw Florizel motioning for a stage employee.

"It appears we have a few minutes before the play starts." He nodded toward Celeste's parents. "Come and let me introduce you to my family."

After the appropriate introductions, everyone settled in their seats. Several actors took the stage.

Malcolm couldn't help but glance at Pelham's box where the duke sat with his sisters, Lady Honoria and Lady Pippa. Lady Grace, Trafford, and Ravenscroft had joined them. Pelham inclined his head and smiled at Malcolm and Celeste. They returned his greeting and then turned their attention to the stage.

The original actors on the stage had been replaced with several others.

"What is going on?" Celeste whispered. "They're running hither and yon with no one seeming to know where their places are." She laughed and leaned close. "It seems you should have left the sticky varnish where it was. At least, the actors would be stuck to the floor, and we could see the play."

He took her hand and interwove their fingers together. "I adore that you always know how to make me feel accomplished."

"Well, you did finish the varnishing formula, and it was a rousing success." She leaned near and lowered her voice. "It's quickly turning into one of your best inventions."

It had been quite a surprising wedding present. He'd

been thunderstruck the second morning after his wedding to wake up with a formula that would work.

"We received another twelve orders through the post today." She sighed slightly. "Is it horrible of me to want to tell Exehill how he was completely wrong about you? You're the definition of success and the hardest worker I know."

A keen sense of satisfaction spread through his chest. He adored that she was involved in his work and wanted to help him in his laboratory and workplace. "You're the hardest worker I've ever had the good fortune to meet." He brought her hand to his lips. "And I'm married to you."

Slowly, a smile spread across Celeste's lips. "I've discovered something about myself since I've married you."

"Tell me." He was always captivated when she talked about the changes in her life since they married.

She sighed slightly as she gathered her thoughts. "I came to the theatre before I had the pleasure of coming to know the real you." She waved her hand across the theatre. "I came here so I could pretend I was another person. I was envious of the characters on the stage."

"You mean the actors?" he asked.

"No." Her brilliant gaze held his. "The characters they portrayed. Those characters had a much more exciting life than I did. But now, my life is full of all sorts of riches, and I'm not talking about money. And it's all because of you."

Malcolm stole a kiss from his precious wife. It was doubtful that anyone noticed. The audience booed and yelled with demands that the play begin.

"Shall we leave, duchess?" Malcolm squeezed her hand with his.

"A brilliant idea, my darling. Grolier and my parents have their carriages."

They quickly said their goodbyes. Once they exited the box, Celeste stopped him with a touch on his arm.

"Malcolm, I don't need to pretend to be happy. I have the best life anyone could want because I have you."

"And I have you, the love of my life." He took her arm in his and escorted her out of the theatre. "Let's go home."

"To see Darling, then to bed?" She waggled her eyebrows as he helped her into their carriage.

"You are a greedy little duchess, aren't you?"

She laughed, then stole a kiss. "You made me this way."

Malcolm kissed her on the tip of her nose. "And I wouldn't change a thing about you. Lucky me."

Want to find out more about the characters in
***The Duchess of Drury Lane*?**
Then you'll want to meet the
Millionaires of Mayfair.

Read on for a preview of **A Simple Seduction**, the first novel in the **Millionaires of Mayfair** series, featuring the Duke of Pelham and his two sisters.

Or visit Janna's website for more information about all her exciting books:
https://www.jannamacgregor.com

SNEAK PEEK: A SIMPLE SEDUCTION
MILLIONAIRE'S OF MAYFAIR BOOK 1

For the first time in her life, Honoria felt beautiful. Completely concealed behind the mask and the burnished blond hair that fell to her waist, she straightened her back and studied the crowd. Men stopped their conversation and stared at her. Their appreciation for her costume made their eyes glint.

As Honoria surveyed the room, more and more men turned her way. Even the women who were attending took notice. Most of the men wore simple black cloaks with a traditional black domino mask, but some were dressed as clowns, jesters, medieval warriors, and even priests. The women were far more colorful in their dress. Shepherds, nuns, and queens of yesterday were all represented at her brother's masquerade party.

She'd changed her simple gown for the costume behind a copse of trees. At first, she'd felt exposed in the costume. With a silk that perfectly matched her skin, Honoria's gown made everyone take a second glance to ensure that she wasn't naked. A golden gaze netting with strategically sewn brilliants and beads covered the gown.

Her every breath made the ensemble twinkle like water drops clinging to her skin.

And there was no one else dressed as her.

Honoria glanced up at the second floor where her brother stood in all his glory, dressed as some Greek god. The pale sheen of his blond hair was unmistakable. Two men flanked him.

She took a breath to summon the fortitude to step into the masquerade. Not a single soul would know her identity. Including her brother. All anyone saw was Venus. A smile creased her crimson-colored lips. Never in her life had she worn rouge on her lips, but her disguise emboldened her. Such confidence gave her the courage to find a lover.

A footman dressed as one of Robin Hood's merry men took her hand and helped her onto the dancefloor. "May I offer something to drink?"

When she shook her head, the footman bowed then left.

As she surveyed the people gaily dancing, the crowd parted, and a man strode directly toward her. He'd been one of the men standing by her brother. The man's height allowed him to see over the crowd. From afar, he walked with confidence. The closer he came, the more defined his features. His gaze locked with hers. His expression was terrifyingly determined and confident. Yet even with his half mask, it didn't hide his square jaw and chiseled cheekbones.

He was the one she would pick tonight.

Her heart pounded in her chest as another idea took hold.

What if Pelham had recognized her and sent the man to escort her to him? In that instant, her best-laid plans of hiding behind a costume seemed outrageous.

The stranger's gaze never left hers as he approached. With his every step, her heart pounded harder and faster. Quickly, she scanned the room for another exit. She would not allow herself to be discovered and face the humiliation of confessing to Pelham.

He'd not understand why she wanted one night of passion and affection before she turned her back on the possibility of marriage. Though Pelham had constantly argued that she was hardly a spinster and highly desirable as a potential marriage candidate for the male paragons of the *ton*, she wasn't for them.

Several couples danced across the floor and blocked the veritable giant from continuing his resolute stride to reach her. Honoria took the opportunity and hurried through a door on the left that led out to a passageway. Once out of the ballroom, she took the first left and found a library of sorts. As her heartbeat galloped through her chest, she tucked herself into a darkened corner next to a bookshelf and waited. Old habits never died. She still had the ability to hide in plain sight.

Slowly, she brought her hand to her chest and breathed as quietly as she could, praying her runaway heartbeat would slow down before it burst through her chest.

No footsteps followed her.

She took a deep breath and relaxed her shoulders. Immediately, she inhaled the scent of oranges and spices. The pleasant fragrance was layered with something darker, and she silently gulped another breath.

She leaned her head against the bookshelf and closed her eyes. She could taste the disappointment that quickly replaced her giddy excitement for a pleasure-filled evening of fun. The man would be looking for her all night. Perhaps it was best if she went home and waited for her brother's arrival. No doubt, he'd summon her to his study tomorrow for a proper lecture.

He'd never chastise Honoria for her actions tonight, but he'd be disappointed in her. That would hurt far worse than any punishment he could inflict.

Why was it that men could enjoy the company of a woman without matrimony, yet a woman couldn't enjoy a man's company without being ruined? Honoria glanced out the window at the star-filled sky. It was such a magical night, but now it held no promise of amusement.

Honoria smoothed her hands down the beautiful gown again. Such a waste not to be able to wear it all evening. She hadn't even had the chance to dance or flirt with a handsome man.

Well, there was nothing to be gained by asking the what-ifs and why-couldn'ts of the evening. Yet, Honoria had stood on the edge of the room and had commanded attention.

Pushing aside her disappointment, Honoria carefully stepped onto the terrace. Once she found the steps that led to the small garden, she carefully gathered up her gown in her hand so she could move freely without fear of falling.

As she lifted her foot to take the first step, a deep masculine voice chuckled. Then a half growl, half whisper surrounded her. "Venus, I was afraid you'd gone back into your shell."

* * * *

When Venus whipped around, Marcus instinctively grabbed her arm to keep her from falling.

Her other hand flew to her chest, and her eyes widened behind the mask.

"Careful. I apologize for startling you." Gently, he released her. "I didn't want you to take a tumble." He offered his most charming smile. "I hope we could spend some time together this evening."

"Do I know you?" Venus asked.

The sweet, silken smoothness of her alto voice sent prickles across his skin. "No. Shall we change that?"

"Perhaps." Her gaze traveled the length of his body then returned to his. "I want..." She shook her head. "Pardon me. I must gather my thoughts. I don't know how to approach the subject, so I'll be direct." A smile creased her lips. "I'd like to spend the night with you. How much does something like that cost? One hundred pounds?"

"You...you want me to pay you a hundred pounds?" Marcus needed a chair before he fell over. Never before had a woman bargained for her favors at such an exorbitant price. But then, he didn't have much practice in this type of negotiation. He didn't have a mistress. Too messy. Nor did he seek entertainment at bawdy houses. This woman was attractive, but one hundred pounds?

Her eyes widened in horror. "Oh no. I'll pay you. But there are no attachments."

"Meaning?" he asked.

"I'll not marry you."

Marriage? Who thought of marriage at a gambling hell masquerade party?

He blinked twice, trying to understand what she was saying. Then it dawned on him that Pelham and Ravenscroft must be behind such a farce. "Did my friends put you up to this?"

Venus frowned. "I assure you this is just between us." She tilted her nose in the air. "But I won't proceed until it's understood that there are no attachments."

He slowly released a breath. What the deuce was she up to? "You think you'll be forced into marriage if we spend time together?"

She cocked her head. "Isn't that normally what happens?"

He chuckled. "At a masquerade?" He chuckled when her brow crinkled adorably. "I suppose if we're compromised and must marry, one of the priests attending tonight can do the honors."

He bit his lip to keep from laughing again. This was not the type of marriage he should be concentrating on. But it was only for one night. Where was the harm? He didn't even have a woman in mind except for perhaps Pelham's odd older sister. The duke didn't seem to care that Marcus wanted to talk to Venus.

She laughed, the sound reminding him of the Christmas bells of his youth. "You're teasing me. The evening grows late." She almost curtseyed, then caught herself. "If you'll excuse me?"

"Wait." He placed his hand on her forearm, stopping her from leaving his side. Was he actually considering her offer? She was unusual in a way he couldn't explain. Yet, there was something about her that intrigued him. "Before I commit to your request, I want to see how we are together. Have a taste of one another."

She stood there, not moving an inch. With her mask, it was hard to read her expression.

"Wouldn't you agree?" He took a step back and waved a hand in invitation for her to join him on the terrace. "Come, Venus."

Eventually, she took a step closer. Her jasmine scent wafted his way. "You're certain you don't know who I am?"

"No. But I would very much like to change that." He inhaled and held her fragrance for as long as he could. Her floral scent was as unique as she was. She was tall for a woman, extremely so. When he kissed her, he wouldn't have to bend in half to meet her lips with his. Quickly, Marcus allowed his gaze to take in her form. Venus's dress hugged every curve of her lithe body. He'd always preferred women who were more well-endowed, but Venus set his pulse pounding.

She studied him as he studied her. After a moment, her brow crinkled. "I've never been to a masquerade before."

"Never fear, Venus. I'll teach you everything you need to know." When she bit her plump lower lip, it took every ounce of fortitude not to lean in and kiss her. His voice lowered of its own accord. "We are all inexperienced at one point in time or another."

Her eyes widened behind her mask. "I—I—"

Damn him to hell. She almost seemed shocked in what he'd said. "I meant as in first-time-to-a-masquerade. My first such party was when I was seventeen and at university."

"How old are you now?" A hint of challenge tinted her voice.

"Thirty. Is that too old?"

She glanced at the steps of the terrace and shook her head. Slowly she lifted her eyes to his, and a broad smile graced her lips. "It's ideal. Like a perfectly aged whisky."

He tilted his head back and laughed. "No one has ever compared me to perfection."

"I didn't say that, good sir." Her lips pursed in a wicked smile. "I believe that no whisky is truly perfection."

Marcus brought his hand to his heart in a mock show of pain. "You wound me, Venus."

"You didn't let me finish," she said softly. "Remember, whisky continues to change in taste as it ages. Just like humans. Perfectly aged is a personal preference, is it not?"

"Oh, Venus, we shall get along very well, I predict." He took a step closer. "You are my ideal of desire."

"How could you know that if you haven't seen me or spent any time with me?" she challenged.

"I know myself," he volleyed. "Therefore, I know what I desire." He slowly reached toward her, then cupped the back of her neck. She inhaled sharply but didn't pull away. "I desire you."

At this very moment, he wanted to tear her mask off and take her into a kiss where they both would lose themselves within one another. He definitely wasn't perfect and never would be. Yet she was interested in him.

"How do we make introductions without revealing who we are?" she asked.

"If you're not comfortable telling me your real name, I can be Adonis to your Venus."

She shook her head. "Their story is sad. Venus begged him not to go hunting because she dreamt that he would be killed. He didn't listen."

"And died when a wild boar attacked him." He'd give anything to see her face at this moment. "Why don't you call me Marcus?"

When she smiled, he felt ten feet tall.

"That's a beautiful name." She cupped his cheek just as he'd done to her. "Call me...Noria."

"Noria," he whispered, then lowered his lips to hers.

She exclaimed softly when he brushed his mouth against hers. It wasn't a kiss per se, but a hello of sorts. He pulled back and studied her gaze. The pounding pulse at the base of her neck drew his attention. God, he wanted to kiss her there. Frankly, there wasn't an inch of her that he didn't want to taste. He leaned in again and angled his mouth to hers. This time he pressed his lips to hers and stayed there. Slowly, ever so slowly, he took her in his arms and brought her close. Through the thickness of his cloak, the hard shells covering her breasts pressed into his chest.

A whimper escaped her.

"Am I hurting you?" he asked softly and took a step back.

"Don't you dare pull away," she exclaimed breathlessly, then clutched his cloak in both hands and brought him closer. "Things are just now getting interesting."

THE SCANDALS AND SCOUNDRELS
OF DRURY LANE

Want to read the next story about The Scandals and Scoundrels of Drury Lane?

Keep reading for The Phantom of Drury Lane by Kate Bateman

SNEAK PEEK: THE PHANTOM OF DRURY LANE

BY KATE BATEMAN

Chapter 1

The Theatre Royal, Drury Lane, London – 1817

Of the many things Lucy Montgomery had missed about England, William Arden, Viscount Ware, had *not* been one of them.

Three years had not been long enough.

Three decades probably wouldn't suffice.

Some men were simply too vexing for words.

Her stomach somersaulted with an unwelcome combination of anticipation and dread as the man in question pushed through the crowd, making a beeline for the quiet corner she'd chosen for herself in Lady Carrington's ballroom.

His desire to torture her clearly hadn't abated during her time abroad.

Lucy narrowed her eyes, studying him as she'd once studied a jaguar in the steamy jungles of Brazil; with the same fascinated wariness. She hadn't seen him since her family had docked in London three weeks ago, and despite her dislike of the man, she could grudgingly admit his physical appeal.

He'd always been attractive, but the scar that now slashed across his eyebrow and cheekbone—courtesy of a French saber at Waterloo—had somehow *improved* his appearance. There was no justice in this world. He'd been annoyingly handsome before; a dark-haired, indolent playboy, but this new imperfection just added an air of dangerous, rugged maturity that had been previously lacking.

Damn him.

Lucy took a fortifying swig of punch and schooled her expression into one of polite neutrality even as her heart beat faster in her chest. She was three years older now. Three years wiser. She'd survived a shipwreck off Madagascar and the snake-infested forests of South America. She could certainly face one infuriating, sarcastic scoundrel in a ballroom.

However handsome he might be.

Still, her stomach tightened as he stopped in front of her.

"Lucia."

He said it the Italian way, as he'd always done. *Lou-chee-ah*. Three syllables, drawing it out like honey gliding from a spoon, and all her good intentions evaporated at the hint of teasing laughter in his gravel-deep voice.

"Don't call me that," she snapped. "It's *Lucy*. Only my mother ever calls me Lucia—and only then if I've done something particularly dreadful."

His dark brows rose in amusement. "I expect you hear it on a weekly basis, then."

She ground her teeth, and the corner of his mouth twitched as if he knew precisely the effect he had on her. Had *always* had on her, ever since he'd first come to stay with her older brother during the school holidays, when she'd been a girl.

She forced a sunny smile. "Not at all. I haven't done anything dreadful for weeks. Months, even."

"Then you're probably long overdue."

An inelegant snort escaped her. "Not me. *Lenore's* the scandalous one."

She tilted her head toward the dancefloor, where her twin sister was laughing up into the face of a clearly besotted partner. "Most people still get us mixed up. Although I don't see why, when we're hardly identical."

"Ah, but I'm not 'most people,' am I? I've never confused the two of you." Arden's mocking expression didn't change, but something flashed in his eyes as he studied her. "You, Lucy Montgomery, are . . . unforgettable."

His deliberate pause—and choice of verb—were hardly flattering, and Lucy tried not to wince at the reminder that he'd been witness to some of her most humiliating childhood escapades. She hated the way he always seemed to be laughing at her.

"Yes, well, I'm a grown woman of twenty-two now," she said haughtily. "I'm past all that foolishness."

It was Arden's turn to snort. "Really? Because the Lucy *I* remember couldn't pass up the opportunity for an adventure. Or refuse a dare."

She lifted her chin and met his eyes, despite the quivery, weightless feeling it always produced.

"Not true."

"*So* true," he drawled. "Which is why I bet you'll be the one to unmask the Phantom of Drury Lane."

Her own brows rose; she was intrigued despite herself.

"The what of where? I'm not up to date with all the London gossip yet. You're going to have to enlighten me."

"It's been the talk of Covent Garden for months. I'm surprised it hasn't reached your ears."

"I don't frequent the area as often as you do," Lucy said sweetly, relishing the way his lips compressed at her saucy inference. Covent Garden was known for its proliferation of brothels and taverns. Arden, she was sure, was no stranger to either. "Lenore mentioned that you were 'particular friends' with an actress?"

Lucy had digested that news with hardly a pang. Arden always had a woman on his arm. He attracted everyone, from dairymaid to duchess, and he rarely denied himself female company. The twinge in her midsection had *definitely not* been jealousy.

He sent her an easy smile. "You're referring to Kitty? Or maybe Barbara? Either way, we've parted company. But that's beside the point. I know the gossip about Drury Lane Theater because I have a financial stake in the place."

"How so?"

"When the previous building burned down, my father donated funds to rebuild it and became one of the major shareholders. He gifted me his stake three years ago. Just after you left for lands unknown."

"Oh."

Lucy couldn't quite hide her surprise. She'd never imagined Arden as having any interest in business. He'd always seemed too carefree to bother with such serious matters, but perhaps he wasn't quite such a dedicated libertine as he'd once been. Perhaps the war had changed more than his physical appearance.

The thought was intriguing, but she quashed it. Leopards didn't change their spots.

"So, tell me about this Phantom, then," she prompted.

Arden glanced over his shoulder and then leaned in, as

if imparting a great secret, and her heart stuttered as she caught a delicious whiff of his cologne.

God, he always smelled delicious. One day she was going to find out exactly which scent he wore and buy a bottle for herself. For no particular reason, of course. She most certainly wouldn't put a drop of it on her pillow so she could breathe it in while she slept.

His broad shoulders blocked out the rest of the room as she pressed back into the corner, simultaneously breathless at his proximity and irritated at herself for such a reaction.

Her body clearly wasn't as discerning as her brain.

"The Phantom is a masked figure who's haunted the theater for months," Arden said. "He sits alone, in the highest box on the left-hand side of the stage. Sometimes he stays for an entire performance. Other times he only appears for a moment, then vanishes before he can be accosted. Everyone's desperate to know who he is. And whether he's real, or an apparition."

Lucy rolled her eyes. "Of course he's real. There's no such thing as ghosts."

Arden raised his brows. "Are you sure?"

"Your 'phantom' is flesh-and-bone, Arden, I guarantee it. But why are you so keen to unmask him? If he's got people talking about the theater, and buying tickets on the off-chance that they might see him, you should be grateful for the free publicity."

He tilted his head in wry acknowledgment. "I can't deny he's been good for business, but it irks me not to know who the fellow is."

"Have you ever seen him?"

"Not personally. But plenty of other people have. The rumor is that he's a veteran, so hideously scarred by a grenade that he wears a mask so people don't scream in terror when they see him."

Without meaning to, Lucy glanced at Arden's own injury, and his lips quirked as he noted the direction of her gaze.

"Do you find *me* hideous now, Lucia?" he teased, clearly unworried about his own scar. "Do I make you want to scream?"

Lucy's heart was hammering against her ribs. His words sounded as if they had another, far more seductive, meaning. How had things suddenly become so intimate? It felt as if they were the only two people in the ballroom.

She clenched her fingers into a fist against the sudden bizarre desire to touch his injured face, and rallied gamely. "Scream? Only in aggravation."

His gaze dropped to her lips. "Hmm."

Heat washed over her skin at the intense way he studied her mouth. She bit her lower lip, suddenly self-conscious, and he let out a low sound that made her belly tingle.

She'd kissed *his* mouth. Just once. Four years ago, before she'd left for Brazil. The shameful episode was etched into her brain. As was the subsequent humiliation.

"You mentioned a bet?" she said breathlessly.

"I did. Kit Hollingsworth is offering a hundred pounds to whoever unmasks the Phantom."

"And you think that person will be me?"

His gaze flashed back up to hers. "I do. Because if anyone loves meddling and mysteries, it's you. You've been back in London for weeks without a scandal to your name, which means you must be desperate for something to do."

Lucy tried not to look interested. She *had* been getting a little bored. Life in the *ton* was so restrictive compared to the wonderful freedoms she'd enjoyed for the past three years, traveling the globe with her intrepid parents.

Still, the fact that Arden knew her well enough to guess that she'd been longing for a challenge was annoying, to say the least. She hated to be so predictable.

She tilted her head and pretended to give the matter serious thought, despite already knowing she couldn't refuse such an enticing challenge.

"Let me just make sure I have this right. Kit Hollingsworth will give me a hundred pounds if I prove the Phantom of Drury Lane is a person and not a ghost?"

Arden nodded. "You must provide a name."

"Very well. It's father's birthday coming up next month. I'll use the money to buy him a new microscope. His favorite one was damaged when we were shipwrecked."

Arden's lips curved at her confidence, and he moved back, giving her some space. The noise of the crowd intruded again. "I wish you the best of luck. When will you start your investigation?"

"As soon as possible." Lucy sent him a questioning glance. "I assume, as one of the theatre's backers, that you have access to the place whenever you like?"

"I have a key to the side entrance, if that's what you mean. But I'm not trusting you with it, Lucy Lockit."

Lucy scowled at the teasing nickname. Lucy Lockit was a character from John Gay's comedy, The Beggar's Opera—the foolish daughter of the fictional warden of Newgate, who stole the keys to free her bigamous, cheating lover from debtor's prison.

"So how am I supposed to investigate, then?"

His easy smile made her feel like she'd walked into a trap. "I'll escort you, if you like."

Lucy blinked. Arden had never offered to take her anywhere before. In the past, he'd gone out of his way to *avoid* her company.

She narrowed her eyes. "You? Escort me?"

He looked almost offended by her skepticism. "Yes, me. We can go tomorrow morning. Hard as this may be for you to believe, Montgomery, but I do occasionally get out of bed before noon."

A sudden, unwanted mental image of him, sprawled in an artfully concealing tangle of bed sheets, heated her cheeks. He sent her an amused, wicked glance, as if he knew precisely the direction of her wayward thoughts.

"I'll be there, I promise," he said. "The entrance for the boxes is on Brydges Street. I'll meet you there at ten."

He didn't wait for her agreement. He simply turned on his heel and walked away.

Lucy watched him leave with mingled relief and regret. Interacting with Arden always left her slightly on edge, but the thought of having something to enliven her day tomorrow was enough to lift her spirits.

Discovering the identity of the mysterious Phantom would be gratifying. But not half as satisfying as proving to Arden that she was a clever, capable woman, and not the foolish girl he'd kissed and then rejected with such obvious loathing three years ago.

Universal link: https://books2read.com/
PhantomOfDruryLane

Visit Kate's Website to check out all of her books or to sign up for her newsletter.

MORE FROM JANNA MACGREGOR

For the latest news and freebies from Janna, sign up for her Newsletter.

Visit https://www.jannamacgregor.com for more information about Janna's books.

ABOUT THE AUTHOR

Janna MacGregor was born and raised in the bootheel of Missouri. She credits her darling mom for introducing her to the happily-ever-after world of romance novels. Janna writes stories where compelling and powerful heroines meet and fall in love with their equally matched heroes. She splits her time between Kansas City and Minneapolis with her very own dashing rogue, and one smug, but not surprisingly, perfect pug. She loves to hear from readers.

For the latest news and freebies from Janna, <u>sign up for her Newsletter</u>.

Visit https://www.jannamacgregor.com for more information about Janna's books. Or click here

If you want to spill the tea with Janna, join her Ladies and Lords of Langham Hall reader group